the
COLONIST

Michael Schmidt

First published in the UK by Frederick Muller Ltd
This edition published in March 1993 by GMP Publishers Ltd
P O Box 247, London N17 9QR, England

World Copyright © Michael Schmidt 1980

A CIP catalogue record for this book
is available from the British Library

ISBN 0 85449 187 2

Distributed in North America by InBook
P O Box 120470, East Haven, CT 06512, USA

Distributed in Australia by Bulldog Books
P O Box 155, Broadway, NSW 2007, Australia

Printed and bound in the EC on environmentally-friendly paper
by Nørhaven A/S, Viborg, Denmark

the
COLONIST

For
ANGEL GARCIA-GOMEZ

For he hath said in his heart, Tush, I shall never be cast down: there shall no harm happen unto me.

His mouth is full of cursing, deceit, and fraud: under his tongue is ungodliness and vanity.

He sitteth lurking in the thievish corners of the streets: and privily in his lurking dens doth he murder the innocent; his eyes are set against the poor.

For he lieth waiting secretly, even as a lion lurketh he in his den: that he may ravish the poor.

He doth ravish the poor: when he getteth him into his net.

Psalm X (6–10)

I.

Often even now when I wake up I think I'm there. I retain
the error a few moments, half-consciously – seem to smell the
conflicting scents and hear the bristling of tropical foliage,
pretend I am not alone in the bed, extend my hand – into a
vacancy, and let my eyes fall open on English daylight.

I still keep the habit of sleeping with the curtains drawn
back and the windows thrown wide, even in winter. I explain
it as a hunger for fresh air. But it is more a chronic expectation, as I lie gazing at the blue or cloudy blank framed by
pelmet, curtains and sill. It's futile as the childhood prayers
of an atheist, which recur to him instinctively and are half
said before he catches himself out. Sometimes an inert white
moon lies against a daylit sky like a tiny cloud without a drop
of water.

In the disorientation of early morning I return there –
because the events were incomplete. It was a place and time
alive as little has been since. I spend hours interrogating it,
like an historian puzzling at a fragmentary chronicle, who
takes the problems home because they will not let him go.
Finally he decides to understand at all costs, if only to be shut
of them at last; he packs away his books, travels backwards
in time, takes boat to the place where the lost events occurred;
– and there, in a suggestive climate, among ruins and citrus
trees, in the dusty roads, among high white-washed rooms,
in the cafés and bars of the descendants – there in the very
face of change – he creates the matter missing from the text.
It is not a form of evidence his professional colleagues would
countenance, but something better, whose truth the pulse
acknowledges, the body understands uncritically, regardless
of disciplines of mind. As he approaches, it recedes, drawing
him further on – and into it, so that in the end he finds an
absence, or himself, or perhaps in a rare moment (and only
for a moment) the thing he sought. He has discovered that
nothing but detail is ever lost for good. The forms survive in
present forms – flawed, and as years pass, the flaws grow

deeper. Nothing changes, each thing becomes in time more itself, defined, uniquely broken.

I find my subject in some photographs, some manuscripts I have here at hand – tangible documents to toy with. They emerge from ten years' life. But the dozen photographs represent only a dozen posed instants of ten years. The tidy manuscripts – containing more time, more substance for reflection – are as self-deceived as the photographs are deceiving.

In other places, I could search him out. Disguised as a researcher, I could interview Doña Constanza, my old nurse – now long-retired – in her two small rooms with the balcony overlooking the *mercado* and the variegated, noisy fruiterers' stalls. Her rooms when I last visited them were pungent with the smell of over-ripeness. She sat, a large figure in a small chair, her tight braids – now grey – wound up on top of her head, nodding and nodding, smiling at me and winking now her white eye, now her good eye. She still talked with me as though I were her charge and looked through me to the child she had tended, until I too could stand aside and regard – in her manner to me – what I had been to her. The past she embroidered in her lovely country Spanish, chuckling especially at the early years, mischievously recalling my infancy. But there were later years whose substance silenced her. Her memory or her voice preferred to pass them over. Her habit was to remember the good times and thank God in every other sentence, as though he too were party to them. He had been invoked then – frequently – and more now. The rosary I gave her one Christmas, which long use had blackened, was clutched in her hands, and the beads passed through and through fingers agile for prayer despite the swollen knuckles.

Or if I knew where he lived I'd no doubt be able to pick the memory of my garrulous religious mentor – my 'catechist' – the Reverend Purse, English rector to the small Episcopalian congregation of the very large parish of San Jacinto. He had been a party – unwittingly – to the forgotten years, with his sanctimonious concern. Where would he be now? Doubtless retired to some English village, enjoying the wet weather he nostalgically evoked when he reclined on a garden chair among his English and American parishioners. Beside their pools, enjoying their casual hospitality in his flowered shirts, short trousers, 'I sometimes feel like one of the natives,' he would say, beaming at the foreign natives among whom he took his untaxing gospel. The wealthy, suntanned businessmen and their wives trusted him. He was among the first to greet them when they took up weekend residence or retirement in the salubrious environs of San Jacinto. The rector would discuss those years with me. He talked about anything. With an ingratiating tilt of the head to one side and a slight impediment, like a wayward lisp, he was the fountainhead of gossip.

There are my parents, too. But I have tried them. They tell nothing. They did not experience the good early years that sustain Doña Constanza. They gave those years to her, renounced them for themselves. It was my delicate health, my own 'good', and simple, sensible expediency that made them relinquish me to her care. And I am not ungrateful to them for it. A sickly child was an embarrassment for a prominent man of business. And his wife could not wear herself out on behalf of a creature who – when they consigned him to the care of Doña Constanza at their weekend house – was not expected to survive. As I grew stronger, my absence was a habit for them. They visited the tropics on weekends, bringing their harsh formality into my world, and never seeking to exist there on any terms but their own. When the problems came, they were angry and perplexed. But the problems passed. In their terms, I have turned out as well as could be expected. After the age of nine, when I was sent away, they had asked very little of me. They provided a house and servants. There was a good English school to see to me, during what they called, even after I was well, my 'convalescence' – seven and a half years of it.

Or, if I could find him, I might question Chayo. If I could find him, though, there would be no need for questions – no need at all.

11

II.

The photographs recall the house itself. Subsequent owners have altered it so thoroughly that only the view is unchanged, and the long lonely track to the gate. The gate is painted scarlet (in my time it was jet black, with a fine outline of white). When I visited five years after my father sold it, it seemed all wrong, another place. The trees near the gate had been felled, the house façade was altered, the front garden was like a barrack yard, cobbled, with wrought-iron tables and chairs scattered about it at attention. I looked for some proof that this was indeed my house, and there suddenly was the view – the same view I had had from my window, across the deep *barranca*, where the river ran, past rice fields opposite to the faceted copper-coloured mountains of Parano, and beyond, ice-blue through the undulating heat, the great peaks of the volcanoes. I took my bearings from them; and as I left I closed my eyes to the altered foreground, the changed house, and was driven back along the half-mile track to the road. For a moment I was again leaving my own home.

The road into town is now paved and lined with dessicated tulipan trees. Behind them, the squatters' hovels have taken on an air of permanence. They are no solider, but weather-beaten now they look like staying. The roadside seems to be lined with naked children, there are so many. The town spreads towards the solitude of what was my house, but stops short over a mile off, leaving what was locally called 'the green island' an island still, surrounded by rough fields and untillable gullies. Sometimes I hope the town will take it in – that island I inhabited with Doña Constanza and Chayo. If the town swallows it, there will at least be no particular place to return to.

Without the aid of photographs I cannot place exactly where the hammock hung and I lay during the early months of my convalescence, watching the mountains for hours. I can't recall where the giant Indian laurel stood near my room. The room has been extended, the laurel downed. Now there are bars on the windows to dissuade burglars. In my time there were no bars on the windows. There were screens, and removable at that. There were thick vines – ficus largely – which you could climb up and down. Now it is stark plaster, painted pink, and the bars painted black – a pseudo-colonial mansion. It is a house for a general: orderly, secure, tasteless.

And the garden, once a series of small terraces descending the steepness to the river, a hundred feet below, has been professionally landscaped, the single fruit-trees downed, large sweeping stairs arranged between massive retaining walls, attempting a Tuscan dignity that terminates its grand lawns and flower-beds at the narrow brown course of the river, frilled with young holm-oaks. The great holm-oaks where Chayo and I suspended our swings and drifted out over the choppy water have been removed to give a clear view of the poor dam, with its continual waterfall sound. The steep scrubby bank and cliffs opposite are unchanged.

Photographs, conversations don't retrieve the moments that I want. The fire. The end of my long convalescence. Why the discretion? My father would offer a severe version, coldly true as to particulars. My mother would tell it more gently, but still partially. The lost years belong to two people, and one of them has disappeared.

The fact that the fire did not burn cleanly away, that no one was clearly punished, means that punishment becomes the long disruption of a life. No ghost is more persistently unsettling than a partial one – neither totally familiar nor altogether strange.

III.

The books are closed, the ship boarded at Liverpool, sailing back to Veracruz, and the train journey to the capital, and the bus over the mountains to the tropics – and all this time the diminution of the traveller – thirty, twenty, eighteen, sixteen, until he's fourteen, in a room with other books – schoolbooks – spread out on a table beneath a window. And from the window (framed with dark-leaved ficus) he can see down past the terraces and treetops the deep gully through which the river cuts, intermittently visible; and beyond that, directly opposite, the rice fields, and the foothills, and at the end of the vista the volcanoes, snow-topped, with no covering of cloud; and the river sound comes through the open window, with the sound too of day-insects, and the clack of secateurs at work in the shrubberies.

Though the door is closed, the droning of Doña Constanza's tuneless song, faint but persistent, finds its way in from where she is cleaning in the next room. It is like the scent of familiar flowers, not sweet but pervasive, assuring. And there is beside the bed, on a large chest of drawers, a chiming clock with its firm, gentle ticking, and the pendulum visible through a little glass panel – a clock the boy winds every Sunday, methodically, when he gets up – a little act of worship. It is his only precious possession. It lives a full week on one winding.

First, there is Doña Constanza. Only, I must translate her grand title and address her as Nana, the name I called her by. As I grew older, she seemed to shrink – but when I was first transported with her to the weekend house, ill and weak, she was a large comforting figure – not quite a mother to me, but in some respects rather more. An electric bell attached my room to hers, so I could call her in the night. She was not young even then, though her hair was black and her portly figure moved animatedly, brisk and graceful in its Indian way. At the least pretext – fear of the foliage brushing the window-screen, distant night-sounds, or some silent fear – I would find my way to her quarters and crawl into her bed

14

beside her. Her rough flannel nightgown and her warm sweet-smelling form released me from any terror. Until the last months of my tenth year I spent many nights in the shadow of her form. It remained somehow patient and attentive to me even as she slept.

My father had employed Nana as a house-maid three years before I was born. She came to his gate in the capital with a child, begging for work. My father gave her employment, lodging and a modest wage. The child went elsewhere.

Soon my mother discovered that the Indian woman could cook and – though illiterate – had an unfailing memory for recipes and instructions. She ceased to be a housemaid and became cook – common Constanza turned into Doña Constanza, who automatically took and expected to take any important duty into her own hands. She made herself irreplaceable in the domestic arrangements of my parents' early marriage.

When I was born, she took me on. I rode inside her knitted shawl and passed my hands across her white eye and her good eye. Sometimes she let down her braids, tying them at the ends with thick woollen string, and let me sit in them as in a swing, riding on her back. When I began to talk – and I learned her language first – she told me of her *pueblo* in simple words: the fields in which she had worked from the beginning, the village not far from the capital, her sisters. Her mother still lived there, a devout old lady I once met at our gate (the servants were not allowed to invite their visitors into the house). Nana had no father, a phenomenon she did not explain to me. Nor did her own child, whom I never saw, have a father. Somehow, her mother had a bit of land and an adobe house hedged in with organ cactuses.

Often she told me the story of the milk-snake. There was, she said, a snake in her *tierra* that lived on milk from the cattle. As they grazed, it would writhe up their legs and fasten to an udder, drawing off the milk until the cow went dry. She said that when a mother fell asleep while nursing, the snake would sometimes come, fasten to the breast and give the baby its tail for pacifier. Then it went away, and the baby died.

She hated the wicked maguey cactuses that abounded on the dry hills and along the edges of the stony fields. From them the farmers took the *agua miel* they fermented into *pulque*, what she called 'the devil's drink'. She would declare that *pulque* had widowed her – but she was not a widow. In unconsidering moments she forgot I knew she had a child. She would refer to herself laughingly as 'señorita', and then blush for reasons I surmised later. She seldom spoke of men – except the saints – and I imagined the smoke rising from small chimneys and the dry fields of a place where only women lived, industrious and virtuous as she now was; with a church whose every detail she evoked for me, so that I could almost feel the chill yellow stone on which she had spent half her youth kneeling in prayer.

Nana took her infrequent vacations making pilgrimages – to Chalma for the indulgence due upon a visit to the Black Christ, to the Basilica to thank the Virgin of Guadalupe for one of the many miracles entreated. She had a knack with the saints: her prayers were always modest and always answered. When she prayed for her animals (she kept birds and two cats) they recovered from their slight illnesses, and the saint was paid with a little silver token. The saints she credited with my own recovery from my early disease. I remember one day during the worst of it waking from a delirious sleep to a terrible scene. Nana had slipped a picture of the Virgin of Guadalupe discreetly under my pillows as I slept, 'so she could be close to you and cure you', she explained. In my restless sleep I had thrown off the pillows and when my mother looked in to see how I was she discovered the picture and called my father. He summoned Nana and I woke with the room full of people. My father was upbraiding her in his severe, quiet voice. 'My son is not a Catholic.' His large hand, trembling with dry anger, held up the little picture before her, then crumpled it up and threw it into the corner. Nana retrieved it later. Only in this respect was she insubordinate. She would not cease to share her saints with me. But from this incident she learned discretion. The image of the Virgin, pressed flat again but ever after creased from its sickbed martyrdom at my father's hand, retained its place in her pantheon. Why should it not? Her faith was efficacious. I have no doubt but that her prayers for the departed were as promptly seen to by the saints as her prayers for the living, beast and man.

She was skilled with herbs as well, so that when I had relapses or small ailments she seldom had recourse to the doctor, but brewed me foul-tasting teas of mamey-skin or concocted some bitter stem or blossom from the garden and made me well in a few hours. Sometimes she did not even trouble my parents, when they came, with a report of my illness. I was her charge, and she saw no need to share me altogether. I was not the sole beneficiary of her medical skills. In time she came to be thought of in the town of San Jacinto itself as something of a white witch, and poor people came down the long track to our gate to beg her remedies, which she gave them, prescribing prayers as well as foliage tea.

Though illiterate, her memory was impeccable. She never forgot anniversaries. Every other day was an anniversary of some sort – of a death, in which case she wore black and a solemn face at breakfast; or a birthday; or a saint's day. Such days had their determined rituals. If it was a saint, she lighted an extra candle in front of her bright little gathering of icons and mementos. They stood on a table beside her bed, dominated by a cheap wooden statue of the Virgin, a foot or so high, protected by a bell-jar and wound round with plastic lilies. Under the bell-jar too she kept the box with her housekeeping money, commended to the Virgin's protection.

My own birthdays and my name days we celebrated in the pantry, eating my favourite dishes. Outside the pantry window were her birds. She had canaries in small square wicker cages, budgerigars in one large wire mansion, and a parrot that disliked her mightily and would peck her hand if she did not grab it first. He was Lazaro, who liked me but hated the rest of the human world. In the pantry, to the constant accompaniment of bird noise, we had our little parties – against my parents' orders, for I was supposed to take my meals in the high, cold white dining room. But when my parents were away I ate with Nana; and later I prevailed on her to let Chayo join us there. The larger of her tom-cats crouched on the window ledge and watched, now the birds, and now the revellers within.

The first two years, apart from school hours, I was hardly away from her. When I was not reading, I would sit on a stool in the kitchen and watch her make tortillas, patting out the fragrant grey corn-dough. We went walks down to the river and collected weeds for her potions. We sang and made up stories. The only language I spoke naturally was hers. My parents, finding fault with my English, complained to the school. But my English tongue was clumsy and thick because

17

I spoke with it only at weekends and in class. The rest of my time I lived another language, and though Nana was no relation of mine, I lived in her world, even if house and furnishings contradicted it. Weekends were times of discomfort. When my father's car disappeared out of the gate each Sunday afternoon, our world relaxed again into its natural state of trust, secure for five days, until again the black gate opened to admit my proper family.

As I grew, my interests ranged more widely. Gradually I withdrew from Nana. I tried to teach her to read and write, so she might accompany me on my intellectual excursions, but the exercise was hopeless. Our classes ended with her telling me stories, or (because the eleven-year-old pedagogue struck her as amusing) laughing me to silence. I would slam out in a temper, or break down in tears of frustration, defeated by what I told her was her stupidity. Humiliated by my attempts, she made excuses to get out of our classes, and at last we discontinued them. She suggested I should read to her, since she could not master the art. I tried this, but with my unerring childish tactlessness I chose the wrong books, and she invariably dozed off. This scheme, too, was abandoned.

The electric bell between my room and hers was hardly used after my eleventh year. Yet even as we grew apart, she remained the organizing principle of our green island. She was the one constant, the point of trust. If I deceived her in anything, I felt I sinned indeed. Though I did not accompany her to church on Sundays, sometimes in the week on special feast-days she took me with her, and merely by the intensity of her observance impressed upon me the morality she believed – utter, unbending, with a terrifying judgement. My lapsed Presbyterian parents knew nothing of these outings of ours. But they knew little of what went on in those years, in their large empty house. They were content to follow the school statistics of my progress, to reprimand and improve my bad manners and my faulty English, trying to polish my social form. For them, childhood was, like my early illness, something to be got over. A decorum developed between them and me. I pleased them as I could by my behaviour and school results. For the rest, I kept myself to myself and Nana.

IV.

I never lacked for books. They were the one pleasure of weekends. My mother always had some new volume for me and my little shelf was too small to contain my library. I ranged the books neatly along the walls, to begin with by height, but later by author.

Books about travel and books about the Conquest were my favourites. I remember particularly a small edition of Exquemelin I was given when I was twelve, and a large volume of *The Discovery and Conquest of Mexico* by Bernal Diaz. I travelled the rough road from Veracruz with the Spaniards – and I failed to connect their Indian victims with Nana's ancestors. It was a story merely, the first times I read it. But a story that stayed with me, and that Chayo explained to me some years later in such bitter terms that I came to distrust the pleasure I had taken in it. For the violent righteousness of the Spaniards that drew my imagination to their heroic deeds had its victims. And, wearing different lives, they still walked their subdued territories, as the conquerors did too, now using more subtle stratagems.

I made do with the idea of travel. All my adventures were vicarious. Nana entertained me with detailed accounts of her pilgrimages. Each shrine had about it a market of a different sort, each had its special miraculous icons and relics. When she went to Chalma she brought me back one of the flower wreathes the pilgrim buys en route, at the mountain spring some miles above the holy town. The wreathes always reached me wilted, but with a priest's blessing and therefore precious. I treasured them until they wilted to twigs. From the Basilica she brought small plastic icons of the Virgin of Guadalupe and of San Martin de Porras. These I hid away where my parents would not find them. From Santo Domingo in Oaxaca one year she brought me a wide cotton belt woven with red and orange crosses. I laid it on the chest of drawers beside the chiming clock. Her travels were always fraught with adventures, since she went by bus, and on her return reported the breakdowns and flat tyres with great enthusiasm; or some small miracle performed on the spot. For a few days after she came back, she was more fervent and vigorous. She could not stop talking. From Chalma she brought always the same story of the Black Christ and told it in the same words, year after year, so I was tempted to forestall her. But I let the story flow – like the story of the milk-snake – and it tempted my faith too.

For my part, I never visited the capital. When I asked if I might be taken, I was reminded of the delicate state of my health. Even when I grew robust and protested, listing the places I wanted to visit in the city, my parents shook their heads. The green island and San Jacinto were my sphere, though after the age of eleven I had no serious relapses.

My spiritual life had little attention until my fourteenth year. Each Sunday, of course, I was driven to church with my parents. I knew the Episcopalian service by heart. No one had challenged me to believe or otherwise, and I accepted it as a social ritual, one of the inevitable discomforts of the weekend. But in my fourteenth year the Reverend Purse mooted first to my mother, then my father, the possibility of my confirmation. And my father, lapsed Presbyterian though he was, saw in the prospect of regular tuition from the Reverend Purse an improvement of my English, and perhaps of my conversation. The clergyman was asked to instruct me at home once a week. The Reverend Purse, my mother liked to say, was 'a godsend' – having the spiritual aspect more in mind, perhaps, than my practical-minded father did. But like his, her religion was more evident in prejudices than in devotions. Discipline, industry – these were the virtues they extolled in their didactic conversation, always modestly commending themselves and their way of life. Values could be measured materially: wealth honestly come by, and comfort, were like tokens of virtue, and useful in making the choice of friends. Similarly, school marks were a crucial measuring stick of my virtue. If I got '10s' I was destined for an identifiable heaven.

When my mother mentioned that the Reverend Purse was not a Presbyterian, my father shrugged. 'In any case, he's English, and he's Protestant,' he said. And well-connected, too. On those grounds he was welcomed at our table, my parents lubricated him well with their imported Scotch. The

Reverend Purse accepted these attentions quietly, as his due. If he was expected to be a Protestant, he would behave like one. The food was good, the drink abundant. And there was, incidentally, a soul to prepare for confirmation, a soul housed in a young body by no means unattractive, a young mind which, hedged about with shyness, seemed none the less to be intelligent. His small social deceit in not disabusing my father was pardonable and would harm no one.

The year before I was born the Reverend Purse had arrived in the country for a brief visit. He had not returned to England since. The then rector of San Jacinto had fallen ill, and Purse offered to stand in. The then rector died, and Purse was left with the parish on his hands. He agreed to stay until a replacement could be found. 'And this,' he used to smile ironically, 'was my mistake. An *excess* of charity is punished by providence, even in a rector. So here I am. The records of my whereabouts must have gone up in the Blitz. I take my exile like Ovid, or one of those ancient Chinese poets sent to the furthest army outpost – for ever.' Then he would recall himself apologetically and declare that exile in San Jacinto had its advantages, especially in the quality of the parishioners. By this sleight of rhetoric he became at once pathetic and ingratiating.

'Only, you,' he would say, addressing me but through me the whole immigrant community, '*you* are here by choice. I am here on orders. For you, it's a place you could get up and leave tomorrow. For me, it's a matter of vocational discipline.' Though I didn't contradict him, I did reflect that I had made no voluntary choice to come to San Jacinto or, indeed, into his reverend presence. Some of the British and American businessmen, too, were like him involuntary exiles, posted to this country by their employers – the great international organizations he once likened to 'lay churches'. Nor did I see my father as a free agent – free to dismiss his four hundred employees and abandon his house and his roots (he had lived in the country from his childhood) and move off. The Reverend Purse sentimentalized the character of his parishioners. It was essential to him that he be allowed to sport this face of resigned martyrdom, no matter how ill it suited him. No one begrudged it him. It was part of his quaintness and beguiling naivety or (if one were less charitably disposed) part of his hypocrisy.

His holiday visit had prolonged itself, then, until the man – hardly young when he arrived – had thickened into an undeniable middle age. He pretended to expect transfer at any moment, and never properly settled himself in the damp, cold rectory, but moved among his predecessor's furnishings and books like a perpetual house-guest. Yet his very impermanence gave him a social *cachet* among his parishioners. He was indulged as one always on the brink of departure. He offered a permanent impermanence, a ready subject for conversation and sympathy.

Even the little Episcopalian church (how he hated the word 'Episcopalian'!) was dowdy and provisional. During the rainy season, year by year, the roof deteriorated. Collections were taken up for its repair, but the work was never seen to. The paint flaked off and fell spiralling on the parishioners, some of whom knelt in prayer, while others squatted Protestant fashion. The Reverend Purse kept a hybrid house of worship. It was as much a social as a religious meeting-place. The Christmas bazaar and Easter fête attracted his largest congregation.

He was an expert bridge-player, which recommended him to my mother. My father enjoyed his scurrilous anecdotes about the hierarchy of the Church back home. Every other weekend he visited our house, at first merely on a social basis, but after my catechism began, ostensibly to give reports on my spiritual progress. Most Thursdays, at four o'clock sharp, he came to instruct me. It began when I was fourteen and continued until my sixteenth year was almost over – indeed, until shortly before the fire, and to within three weeks of the laying on of hands that all his expense of energy, pedagogic and gastric, had led towards. But no Bishop ever called God to 'regenerate this thy servant by Water and the Holy Ghost', nor to forgive my adolescent sins, though I remember the service, which we studied syllable by syllable, even now.

At four, his little white Hillman would toot at the gate and be admitted by Chayo. Nana – who despised the rector for his pink-rimmed eyes and flowered shirts (and his eager consumption of alcoholic beverages) – brought him a tall glass of iced tea. Invariably he returned this, with a request for whisky and water instead. Nana gave him as slight a measure of whisky as she dared – what was minimally commensurate with civility – and a great deal of ice and water. It was replenished reluctantly by her several times as the afternoon tutorial wore on. To her the man of the cloth seemed a transparent charlatan.

Normally – except on holidays, when his visits were particularly unwelcome – I arrived late. The taxi which brought me home from school every day invariably met 'hold ups' in the sleepy afternoon streets of San Jacinto. I didn't mind. I arrived unhurriedly at about a quarter past four to face the invader of my island. I disliked him as much as Nana did, but for less specific reasons.

'Punctual again I see, boy,' he invariably greeted me. Then genially, confidential, holding up his glass, 'But Doña Constanza has looked after me!' He swirled the pale cold beverage in the sun. Then he propped his naked pink elbows on the glass-topped table and waited for me on the verandah while I changed my school books for my religious books. He gazed vacantly at the view through his faded eyes. In later years I might have pitied him, but at that time I knew only how to despise such people.

'That's a sensible school uniform,' he'd comment wryly when I re-emerged with my Bible, prayer book, concordance and notebook, to settle stiffly opposite him on a straight chair. I wore the regulation white shirt and trousers and shiny black shoes. 'White for boys – it's a bit silly, at a time when you spend three quarters of your life playing.' He would glance down at his 'sensible' attire: the flower patterned shirt and, through the table's glass top, at his knees poking out of Bermuda shorts, at the sandals on his sockless feet. His skin never tanned in the sun but turned pink or simply raw. On a nearby chair he had propped his walking stick (something of an affectation for a man who walked so little) and on it he hung his battered Panama hat. They completed his ecclesiastical garb. 'Each of them being decently habited' said one of the service rubrics . . . but that was for the ordination of deacons.

Eyeing me with a dull, off-putting approval (he often closed his soft hand on my wrist when I answered a question well) he proceeded with his gradual examination of the Creed, Articles and services. He seemed to relish the time spent, however uncomfortable I was. He lingered and laboured points of great simplicity. He digressed when he could and reminisced. My occasional questions or manifestations of boredom startled him back into the ill-remembered alleyways of theology.

The subject came to seem superior to the instructor. He appeared more a hindrance than a guide. In my spare hours I would study by myself, as much as possible without reference to his version. I thought myself deep in the matter of religion, though instinctively I inclined more to Nana's efficacious faith, for all its mystery and irrationality, than to the rector's tidy formulations. He exhausted each point of the Creed with such reductive arguments that it became schematic and incredible, an elaborate, inhuman construct of language logically deployed so that mystery and transcendence could find no chink through which to enter and reassure the spirit. And yet the rector's visits, and every day spent at the English school, removed further and further from me the possibility of Nana's simple, unarguable faith. My own belief became a desire to believe. It was mediated through so many interpreters – in books, at school, at catechism – that at last it became attenuated, intellectual, and finally irrelevant. Nana should have been my model. But she was unable to articulate her faith, and at that time I trusted only what could be translated into words. I outgrew the rector's form of faith, and lost the directness of access to faith which Nana enjoyed. But this came later. My catechist merely helped prepare that route for me.

V.

When the Reverend Purse began his visits, I had already known Chayo for five years. As soon as Nana and I had been despatched to San Jacinto to benefit my health, my father instructed her to employ a gardener. The broken-down gardener's shack near the main gate had long been untenanted, and the grounds had been kept in a sort of order by a succession of unsatisfactory *peones* who, because they were paid a derisory wage and ill-supervised as well, were always found wanting and dismissed. My removal to the tropics and Nana's formidable presence there as supervisor offered an opportunity for getting the place in order. My father bought a field adjacent to the main fruit orchard and briefly entertained plans of extending the rows of trees into the harsh new soil. The new orchard was never planted, but the field proved a rich quarry, later on, for Chayo's and my scorpion hunts. Each large stone harboured a cool patch of damp, a few grubs, and a tense, fast scorpion under its sun-hot surface. Chayo would catch them and deftly break off the sting tip of the tail with one of the sharp flints that littered the ground. He would let the disarmed scorpion flail about harmlessly in the palm of his hand. It was a trick I never tried to master.

Nana gave the gardener's job to a mason who came one day to mend a faulty cistern. He was Don Alegundo, a man not old but without teeth, with watery, deferential eyes and a stoop which made him look frail – though he was in fact tall and strong. He was not industrious, Nana soon discovered. But she pitied him. His wife had deserted him; and not only had she gone: she had left their child to him as well. The child was two when its mother disappeared. Seven years had passed since then, and when Don Alegundo moved into the gardener's shack near the gate he brought the boy with him. My father protested, but Nana stood her ground, remembering her own child exiled by my father's discipline. She argued that there were no relations to take the boy, that his place was with his father, and – the argument which perhaps swayed my father most – the boy would be a useful assistant

25

to the older man in the garden, a sort of apprentice, unpaid and willing.

When Don Alegundo arrived, I had just passed the crisis of my illness and lay exhausted in my room. It was still an unfamiliar place. I gazed out the window and waited for Nana to come entertain me. She spent a long time describing our new world to me in minute detail, so that when I stepped out at last into the brilliant sunlight it was a familiar place, and seemed to be her creation, she had reported it so accurately. When I was still bed-ridden, she put a cause to all the sounds I heard: the river, the insects, the birds. She told me episode by episode about the appointment of Don Alegundo, her argument with my father, the arrival of the new gardener and his boy at the gardener's shack. I asked her to bring them in to meet me. But such people, she told me, could not set foot in the house. What would my father say?

A day or two later, lying under the sheets, still too listless to read, and perspiring in the heavy heat that filled the room, I heard the clicking of secateurs at work on the vines outside my window, low down at first, and then gradually ascending, until the ficus shoots beneath my window began to twitch and drop away. I clutched the sheet at my throat and watched the window. An unknown at work: a healthy one, a strong one, without a face. The shoots trembled and dropped as of their own accord, but there was a low sound of whistling, light breathing, and clipping, clipping. The small crown of a hat appeared over the ledge; then the brim, and the clipping stopped. A face – a mere silhouette against the bright sky – peered in at the window stealthily. It was Don Alegundo's boy, curious about the contents of the house whose outside he was barbering. Within the silhouette I could detect only the shine of eyes – no feature at all.

My room was dim and his sight adjusted only gradually; the white sheet on the bed must have come clear to him. He seemed suspended there a long time, staring in, but it can have been only a few moments before he discerned eyes peering back at him, large with fear, out of the darkness. When he discovered himself watched, he dropped away as though he had not been there at all, so that I almost doubted that I was awake. Later, I heard the pruning secateurs at work further off, no longer near my window. In the afternoon, I got out of bed and tried to catch a glimpse of him, but he kept in close to the house. I could see only the occasional bobbing of his back as he collected the pruned vine shoots and carried them off to the mulch heap.

He fascinated me, even as he terrified me. If I heard him whistling or working near my window, I would get out of bed and stand close by the wall, looking aslant through the screen to see him without being seen. But I witnessed little. Nana told me only that he was 'a good boy, hard working' – nothing more. His father, however, was a subject she soon grew eloquent on. After three days she came into my room in a fury to announce he was a drunk and a layabout. She had surprised him twice asleep under the same tree in the orchard, a bottle by his side. The first time she woke him and he abused her. For the time being she would let him sleep. But she would get back at him. Her plans to confront him with 'himself', as she put it, occupied her mind so fully that she had little attention to spare for the boy who did his father's work.

As strength returned to me, Nana urged me out of doors. I resisted. I was afraid of the drunk man and his boy. But one morning Nana hung the hammock near the house, came and dressed me, and ordered me into it. She wrapped me in a cotton blanket, gave the hammock a small push, and left me clutching a book and contemplating the mountains, in the unfamiliar garden. It was there that I met Chayo.

But first I met Don Alegundo. I had scarcely found a comfortable position in the hammock when he came sidling to the house, carrying in some vegetables for Nana. Seeing the small bundle in the hammock, he approached me, removed his hat very respectfully, and addressed me as 'patron' – a diminutive and pale patron to this swarthy man. He wore a torn khaki shirt that showed half his full brown chest, and his dusty forearms were thick and strong. Hunched though he was, it was not with physical deformity nor with the weight of the vegetables he was carrying, but with a kind of resignation that prevented him from walking upright. I had never seen anyone so powerful-looking or so ugly, moving with languid servility across the tidy lawns like a domesticated ogre round a prince's palace grounds. Some European blood must have mixed with Indian blood to make him. His eyes were blue, and despite his black hair he had pale eyelashes.

27

And his eyes were watery, as if his European part lamented its presence in a native body. He frightened me so much that I could find no word to say to him when he approached. I could not even extend my hand. He stood looking down at me in the hammock. He ran the tip of his tongue along the brush end of his moustache. Then he shrugged, and slouched off. I called for Nana and was taken indoors.

She compelled me out again the next day. I lay stock-still in the hammock, attempting to be invisible, should Don Alegundo pass that way again. I lay with my eyes closed, willing myself no larger than one of the folds in the hemp hammock – absent to the casual eye. But after a short time I heard footsteps purposefully approaching where I lay – light steps. And I opened my eyes. A boy's face appeared over the hammock rim. It looked timid, and that gave me sufficient courage to return the gaze. 'Doña Constanza,' a whisper said, 'told me to greet you.'

I struggled to sit up in the hammock. I extended my hand to him. 'I am Jesus Rosario, at your service,' he repeated the formula, ignoring my hand and bowing his head. 'My father calls me Chayo.' I drew in my hand and watched him. Occasionally he glanced up from under his hat-brim. I said my name and asked if I too was to call him Chayo. He nodded. There was nothing more. I subsided back into my hammock and he disappeared.

At first I forgot him. It was a relief to have got the introduction over. But the impression of his shy face over the edge of the hammock kept returning to me. I began to wonder what he made of me, wrapped in a blanket and rocking back and forth while he worked. I wanted him to approve of me. And I reflected that he was almost as alone as I on the green island. I started plotting ways of getting to know him – putting myself in his way, summoning him to me (for had his father not called me *patron*?), visiting the gardener's shack. But the prospect of bumping into his father dissuaded me. When we at last became friends, it happened naturally and unexpectedly.

As I recovered, I began to walk about the upper garden. Then I made little forrays down the *barranca* towards the river, exploring the lower garden level by level. I encountered Chayo on these walks, but as I drew near his place he would vanish. At last I got as far as the river, and thereafter every day went to the waterside and climbed one of the giant holm-oaks that branched out above the brief length of rapids. I sat there and was cool each afternoon. Sometimes I carried a book, but more often I merely perched on the long rough bough and watched – from a spot where I was hidden – the water, the leaves, and the cliff opposite where several types of bird swooped through the isolated swarms of insects.

Sitting in my secret place one day, I saw Chayo come down to the river. It was his free afternoon. Over his shoulder he carried a long coil of rope. Halting some yards down-river, he chose a sturdy limb and tossed the knotted end of the rope over it, shinnied up and secured it, then descended. In five minutes he had made himself a swing. When it was ready, he climbed up on a high mossy rock, crossed himself, and without further hesitation jumped and floated high out over the river. He made his flight several times, holding on with one hand and stretching the other out to touch the leaves of the trees on the opposite bank. All the while he whistled loudly or in his imagined privacy shouted to the air.

I came down from my tree and took him by surprise. But we were outside the constraints of my house and grounds. He was not shy here, by the river. He was free for the afternoon, with the frayed rope in his hand. I looked on from the bank until he persuaded me to climb the high stone and grip the rope myself. 'We'll go together!' he said, and fixed his grip above my own. We flew out over the water, and I too began shouting and laughing. Then I swung out by myself and he caught me when I drifted back. We took turns or swung together, until I was so weak with exhaustion that he had to help me climb the slope to the house. Thereafter we were friends.

It was a friendship which my parents seemed to approve. They saw me rapidly grow strong. I spent most of the day out of doors with Chayo. My mother would tell her weekend guests, 'The gardener's boy worships him', and I would clench my toes tight in my shoes with mute indignation. I did not contradict her. She was pleased. Health, like school marks, was a measurable accomplishment, and with Chayo I grew healthy.

I did not contradict her for one reason. I felt the frailty of my situation. I did not wish to endanger my friendship with Chayo. It was always under threat from Don Alegundo's bad conduct. If he left, his son would go as well and leave my world unpeopled. I was silent, tactful and worried.

In time, the sun turned me almost as brown as Chayo himself. My main triumph was to convince Nana to break a sacred rule of my father's and let Chayo join us in the pantry on weekdays for lunch and dinner. It was a very special privilege, she told me, and she reminded him that it was an honour with every other mouthful that he ate. His manners improved. He learned to eat with a spoon.

VI.

Don Alegundo stayed with us a year. I seldom saw him. I avoided him by avoiding the orchard where he slept most of the day. But Nana did not avoid him. At eleven every morning she went grimly in among the fruit trees and berrated the poor fellow. At last, tired of being bullied by her, Don Alegundo one sober evening left – or rather, disappeared. He vanished without trace. The police were informed but they of course found nothing. The earth might have swallowed him, and with him all the things he took with him from the gardener's shack: everything but the bed and battered chest of drawers. He managed to cart off even the mirror and the shower fixture. Neither was replaced.

But to my relief, he did not take his son. The boy, originally deserted by his mother, was now effectively an orphan. He knew – or told – nothing of his father's departure. My father and the police asked him a few questions. Nana, in a spirit of thoroughness, grilled him mercilessly. But he said nothing. When Nana charged him with unnatural lack of feeling because he showed no regret at his father's desertion, the boy lost his temper with her for the first time. How could she call Don Alegundo a father, he demanded. The drunk man whom Nana called to judgement every morning was not a pitiable creature whose wife had left him but a cruel man. Later, Chayo told me how his father beat him for no apparent reason, then fell into delirium and woke with no recollection of his cruelty. He compelled the boy to do a man's work, then kept the wages for himself. Chayo did not regret his solitude. His abiding fear was that his father might return.

Don Alegundo's flight occasioned so much trouble that my father decided not to replace him. He ordered Nana to return to the old manner – to employ part-time *peones* and to keep a strict eye on them. But the next weekend he found Chayo still there, living in the gardener's shack and busy about the garden.

'Constanza,' he said, 'I cannot have a child doing a man's work. He'll have to go.'

31

'But he has no place to go. He has no relations.'

'Am *I* to keep him, when his natural parents have deserted him? We'll have to arrange for him to go into an orphanage in San Jacinto.'

'He works well. He works better than a man,' And then cunningly, Nana – knowing how to get her way in this – added, 'And he costs less to hire, too. He works like a man, but he's a boy and earns a boy's wage.' That settled it. She had preserved Chayo for her own peace of mind – he was biddable and he did not drink. But she kept him there for my sake, too. He was an irreplaceable part of our life. So he stayed, earning half what his father had.

Nana and I decided that Chayo ought to have some schooling. I spoke to my father about sending him, even if only to night school. But my father laughed. 'The boy's a gardener by trade. He doesn't need school so much as experience of the ground. And he gets that here. He's got the orchard, lawns, vegetables, flower gardens, even a little topiary to see to. This place is the best school for him.'

My father would not bend. The more I argued with him, the more he laughed at me. The plan was not worth serious consideration. Well – if he would not act, I must. For had not Chayo as much a right to reading and writing as I did? And he wanted to learn. In my indignation, I brought out of my cupboard the teaching aids I had purchased earlier in the year for my attempt to educate Nana. There was a little blackboard, some exercise books for numbers and calligraphy, and a few elementary texts. During the afternoons, after school and during the holidays, I set up class on the lawn beneath my window. Chayo learned rapidly. Soon he could read passably and write with sufficient clarity for me to be able to read and correct his orthography. Education became our favourite form of play. We neglected our adventures along the river and sat in the sun puzzling over our rudimentary lessons.

Nana came out to watch us late in the afternoon. She was proud of me – so proud that at last, perhaps against her better judgement, but she could not resist her enthusiasm – at last she boasted of our classes to my father. He summoned me to him. Without a word, looking hard into my eyes, he struck me on the ear. 'Bring me your teaching toys,' he commanded. I brought the little blackboard to him, and then the exercise books and texts. He took them away. His only explanation was, 'I will dismiss the boy if this continues. He is a gardener. Remember that. You have better things to do with your time than waste it on the servants.'

Then the change began. It was tyranny, I told Nana. And I went to Chayo and told him what had happened. We could hardly comprehend it. Nana dared not agree with me, though she could not disagree. 'Your father knows best,' she said, and she would not let me continue with my classes during my parents' absence. The distance between her and me widened, even as Chayo and I drew closer, compelled together by our grievance which we could refer to no one. Chayo would have surrendered bitterly. But I intended to continue his education by some secret scheme.

I meditated plan after plan. And one night an idea came to me. I climbed out of bed and with my battery torch went to the window. I examined the frame of the screen. It was fixed in place with short nails. The wood was soft and slightly crumbling with *polillo*. I used my pen-knife to work loose one nail after another until I managed to pull away the frame itself. It fell into the room, and the whole night seemed to enter with it. Mosquitoes and moths that – drawn by the light – had been hurling themselves at it found themselves released into the bedroom atmosphere. They buzzed about the night lamp and about me. The stars and moon, no longer veiled, burned brighter. The room annexed itself to the garden. Scents came in with the insects – florifundio, jasmine. I peered over the window sill. The ficus vine branches were strong there, adequate for foothold. I had found the route by which our studies could continue. By night, by battery torch-light. It would be an adventure, and a righteous crime against my father's tyranny.

Next morning I went into the garden directly after breakfast. I sat in a deck chair with a book, pretending to read – but, with the excitement, the words meant nothing. I was eager to break the plan to Chayo.

He came sweeping the lawn with his long twig broom. He worked his way towards me slowly, brushing before him a tide of fallen bougainvillia blossom and laurel leaves, until he was sweeping beneath my chair.

'Up with your feet.'

33

'Chayo, I've got a plan.'

'Move your feet or I'll sweep you too,' he said, waving the broom over me and trailing a long string of grass across my face.

'I have a plan.'

'I have a headache.'

'We can continue our studies.'

'How?' His tone changed to a great eagerness. I told him about the loosened screen. His face fell. 'You can't expect *me* to come into the house! If Doña Constanza found me there, I'd be for it.'

'She won't find you. It will be after bedtime. I'll lock the door.'

'She'll see the light.'

'Not on her side of the house. Besides, we'll draw the curtain.'

'The light shines through the curtain.'

'Don't worry, we'll find a way. We have to start again soon or you'll start forgetting all you've learned already.'

'Professor,' he bowed low, 'I am at your service. When do we begin?'

'Tonight.'

'*Tonight*?' he repeated, startled. He had not expected me to act quite so briskly.

'You can get in through the window. I've prepared it. You just climb up the vines and tap the screen. I'll remove it, and in you come. *Then* we'll work out our strategy.'

Nana appeared on the verandah with a duster. She was wearing black and a severe face. Today was one of her dark anniversaries. Chayo addressed himself to brushing the lawn with extra energy, sweeping away from me until she disappeared. Then stealthily he came back in my direction, ushering the purple wave of fallen blossom before him. 'It's not a good idea,' he whispered. But I would hear no objections.

'We'll go on with the Conquest, shall we?' I spoke under my breath, too. The secret was delicious. We would go on with the history schoolbook, with me reading and him interjecting wry asides, or occasionally reading himself, struggling bravely through the jungle of words and names. 'We broke off at the Conquest.'

'More about Cortez's woman, Malinche!' he exclaimed near my ear.

'More about the expeditions,' I said, pushing his head away. He dropped the broom and grabbed the back of my chair, overturning me on to the lawn and sending my book into the shrubbery. Then he sat squarely on my chest, the damp cuffs of his worn trousers brushing my face. Pensively, his head cocked ironically to one side, he made his fingers into a broom and brushed them back and forth across my face.

'More about Cortez's woman,' he repeated decisively. I rolled him off and we struggled on the lawn until he pinned me again in the same position as before. He tore a handful of grass out of the deep lawn and scattered it onto my face, then leaned forward and blew it off.

'Nana is coming!' I shouted. He leapt up, took his broom, and rapidly gathered the blossom into a hemp sack. Nana stood on the verandah, turning her mournful face towards us. I retrieved my book from the shrubbery. On his way past me, I whispered, 'Tonight!' and he fled from the upper garden.

VII.

I wish I had a good photograph to refer to. I cannot clearly remember Chayo's face, except as it appeared the last night, by the light of the fire. That image seen only once supplanted all others. In those years we both changed considerably, but though the child and adolescent features elude me, I could recognize him in an instant in the street.

There is one photograph, but his straw hat is drawn down, the brim shades the eyes, so he could be anyone – standing beside me, upon whom no shadow falls, tanned like a tropical mariner, my hair bleached to yellow blondness by the sun. Both of us fifteen then, and Chayo already obscure.

I recall his way of laughing. His face would contort as if with pain, his brown eyes sparkle, and his whole body shake, until the laugh at last broke out loud and hoarse. Whenever he spoke, his whole body was involved in the articulation. He seemed to vibrate with thought and then spill his words whether they were ready or not. He had broad, full lips, and none of the diffused European features that had marked his pale-eyed father. But the whole face, though I recall the features, I cannot assemble as it was.

Five years before that photograph was taken, Chayo arrived for his first secret lesson in my room. I heard foliage rustling, then his fingernail drawn sharp across the screen like a match along a matchbox – I half expected a spurt of flame. I jumped out of bed and removed the screen as I had the night before. Mosquitoes and moths came first. Then Chayo, who a year before had peered up over the ledge into my mysterious sick room, climbed into the house for the first time. He was tense with excitement as we talked in whispers, putting the screen back in place. It was a chilly night.

'Take off your shoes and get in here.' I drew back the bedclothes.

'I'm muddy.'

'Don't get under the sheet, then. Slip in between the blankets. There.'

'How are we to read in the dark?'

'Under the blanket. I've got a torch.'

'But Doña Constanza will find out. I'll get the blanket dirty.'

We puzzled about this for a moment. Then he removed his muddy trousers and we both climbed in under the blanket with my battery torch and the schoolbook about the Conquest. 'I'll read tonight,' I said. 'You relax and listen.' I flashed the torch into his grinning face. 'That'll blind you. Now, *attend*, young man. We will begin again, where we left off.' I opened the book. 'Wait!' I reached out to the table beside the bed and got my glasses. I adjusted them low on my nose in a schoolmasterly fashion, shining the light into my own face so Chayo could appreciate his teacher's expression. Then I beamed the light on the page. It was a passage quoted from Bernal Diaz about King Moctezuma.

' "Moctezuma," ' I read, ' "was about forty years old, of a good-height and well-proportioned, without excess of flesh, not too dark of hue but the proper colour and hue for an Indian, and his hair was not too long, but just covered his ears, and his beard was sparse and dark, and his face somewhat long but cheerful, and his eyes well set, and he showed in his person and in his aspect love when it was right to, and gravity at the appropriate time; he was very clean and polished and bathed once a day, in the afternoon. He had many women for friends, daughters of his lords. . . ." ' We paused to discuss this testimony. How, I asked, could the Spaniard describe his victim and his enemy with such sympathy? Chayo did not answer. He always grew restless at the mention of women. At that time the romance of conqueror and conquered interested him far more than the great battles or the long consequences. We paused a while after the mention of Moctezuma's harem. I was more interested in drawing for Chayo a lesson from the great King's personal hygiene.

'He bathed once a day,' I remarked pointedly.

'Probably to be clean for his women.'

'He had the great springs of Chapultepec for his baths. You'd be better if you followed his example.'

'I can't very well, can I? I haven't the great springs of Chapultepec at my disposal, do I! In fact, I haven't even got a shower. My father took the shower fixture with him. And your father hasn't put one in its place.'

'Is there *no* water in your house?'

'A rusty brown trickle comes out the shower-pipe. I rinse there on Sundays before going to church with Doña Constanza.'

'But where do you *bathe*?'

'Well, nowhere. The river is full of mud.'

'After the garden, you smell. I'm half suffocated under here with you.'

He remained silent. I flashed the torch into his face. He was frowning. 'I know! You must shower here when you come in for your classes. Then we won't have to worry about getting the place dirty. Each evening,' I said magisterially, establishing the regulations of our little college, 'you will come in, shower, and then our studies can begin.'

'So, I smell, do I?'

'Only of work. You've been all day in the garden.' I threw back the blanket to admit the fresh, cold night air. The scents from the garden tempered the smell of Chayo. He had too few clothes to change them regularly, too little time and water to wash his linen. I climbed out of bed and went to the chest of drawers. I explored with the torch. 'Take these,' I said, handing him some of my own underwear and socks. He rolled them into a bundle in the dark. I found him a shirt as well. We were the same size: he small for his age because of his poor childhood diet, and I because of my illness.

Our class lasted an hour and a half according to the chiming of the clock.

'It's time you were going.'

'I've never seen your room in daylight, properly,' he said, stretching out full-length on the bed.

'It's not much of a room except the view.'

'I've got the same view from my window, over the *barranca*.'

It wasn't there now. All we could see, since the moon had set, was a few tentative stars. The sky was suffused with that little light that even the darkest nights have, so that the window was a square a little paler than the pitch black walls, and a few shoots of ficus cut into the paleness and wavered with the breeze. There was never silence there except before storms. It was the crickets this night, as other nights, in the rainy season, it was the frogs. Chayo buried his face in the pillow and inhaled. We lay there silent for some time.

'This is a soft bed.' And then, speculatively, he added, 'the covers are scented.' Then he recoiled, as if afraid he'd spoil them with himself.

'No one will notice,' I said. I felt him slipping out of bed, climbing into his trousers. 'I'll dig out some trousers for you, too, tomorrow. Only you mustn't wear the clothes I give you when my father's here.' He shuffled his feet into his sandals. They clicked quietly on the tile floor. 'You see how easy it is to go on studying? It will work fine. No one can stop us now.'

'Where shall I wash tomorrow?' he asked. I took him into the bathroom, where a night-light always burned. He looked about him, and carefully into the mirror. 'My father took the mirror from my house.' He surveyed the tooth-brushes, fingered the plastic shower curtain, the soap, the towels.

'It's time you got some sleep,' I said.

'You mean, you want to go to bed.' He disappeared abruptly through the bedroom window, leaving me to replace the screen.

The next evening, after Nana had cleared away the dinner things and I had accompanied her in her devotions (it pleased her to have me kneeling mute beside her), I retired early to my room and locked the door. Rummaging through my closet, I found trousers and a jacket suitable for Chayo and bundled them together. I did not choose out the best or the most worn, but what seemed to me might please him. Then I drew a chair up to the table beneath the window and prepared the evening's lesson. As the clock chimed nine times, I changed into my pyjamas, climbed into bed and turned the light off.

A few minutes passed. Then came the scratching at the screen. Chayo climbed silently into the room. He handed me a rough bundle.

'What's this?'

'My towel and things.' I led the way into the bathroom. The dim night-light projected our huge shadows against the wall. His towel, when I unfolded it, was damp and ragged.

'An antique. This won't do at all. Wait,' I commanded. I quietly unlocked the door of my room and sneaked into the tall corridor beyond, to the linen closet. I removed a larger soft bath-towel from deep in the pile of towels. It was a petty burglary: my first. I crept back to my room and locked the door.

Chayo had undressed. He stood shivering – with the cold,

not from shame – on the bare tile floor of the bathroom. He took the towel from me and held it to his face, inhaling the clean smell. 'That's your towel, now. Throw away this old rag. And I've got some trousers for you, too, and a jacket.'

I drew aside the shower curtain and turned on the water, adjusting the temperature. 'It's warm!' Chayo exclaimed. I wondered if he had ever had a hot bath before in his life. I stood aside and pushed him in, drawing the curtains to behind him.

'Now wash until you're a new person, dirty friend,' I said. I leaned against the sink to wait for him, but in a matter of seconds he reappeared, declaring himself clean. 'Not yet,' I said, and drove him back inside. Again, almost immediately, he emerged, glistening in the pale light. 'Have you used the soap?' No, he had not used the soap. He didn't know whether he should. 'I'll show you what a bath is! If you won't wash yourself, I'll wash you.' I stripped off my pyjamas and shepherded him protesting back under the shower head. I took a face flannel, dabbed it with soap, and began to scrub him. He struggled for a time until, gasping, I reckoned he was clean. 'Except your hair,' I said, and made him hold still while I lathered it for him. Then we emerged from behind the curtain once again. 'Your education is no easy matter, young man,' I said as we were drying. He was busy relishing the soft towel, which he handled with great reverence, dabbing his face with it but reluctant to spoil it on his wet body or his hair.

I had not seen before another person naked, nor anyone uncircumcised. He looked like one of those statues, only he wasn't white. There was a substantial completeness about his form, a thrifty strength. He seemed to have weight and energy, while beside him my bones felt light as bird bones, my limbs were conscious only of their frailty. 'Dry yourself,' I said, gazing at him. I set an example of how to dry the hair, the back. At last he wiped the steam from the mirror and regarded himself. I watched over his shoulder. He took my comb and ran it through his hair, finding a new parting and watching his face as he played with hair styles. 'We're losing time! It's already half past,' I said. And the clock chimed.

Padding into the bedroom on bare feet, he said, 'That was good.' He sat on the edge of the bed. 'What are we doing tonight?'

It was astronomy. I had already taught him the planets. 'Do you remember them?'

'Mercury, Venus, Earth, Mars, Jupiter, Saturn, Uranus, Neptune and Pluto,' he exclaimed in one breath.

'Well.'

He climbed in between the blankets. 'No, it's alright now. It's between the sheets.' Delicately he drew the top sheet back and shivered as the cold, smooth fabric received his naked body. 'Shove over,' I said, and climbed in too. Once under, in our restricted classroom, I unfolded my little chart of the stars and with the battery torch we surveyed the heavens there. It was difficult not to be always getting up again to consult the night sky. But we kept our study under covers, afraid of making noise or showing lights. Suspense and proximity facilitated our learning. We were conspirators. In a short time we understood the disposition of the skies on paper. The names were magical. We folded the star map away and said the names over by turns. I had spent time in our earlier classes telling Chayo classical legends – though not to prepare him for astronomy, which did not interest me until he asked about it. But now we lay back embroidering the myths that gave their names to the constellations and single stars. I asked him to recall Andromeda. The myth came from him in a variant form, no longer classical but Indian, the characters transposed into another world. He had appropriated them.

The clock chimed eleven. Then eleven thirty. But the class proceeded. When we fell silent at last, around midnight, Chayo did not get up to go. He lay there. I thought he was dozing.

'Class dismissed!' I jabbed him in the ribs.

'It's very comfortable here.'

'You'll be back tomorrow.'

'My house is – far away.' He yawned enormously and turned over on his side, his back towards me, as though he intended to stay.

'You can't spend the whole night here!'

'Oh,' he said dejectedly. He put his foot out of bed and sat up. 'It's too much, I suppose. I was thinking of the room I live in.' I considered. How, too much? Our conspiracy was already enormous. His small house, without a mirror or a shower, haunted by vermin, seemed remote and hostile. I'd never been inside it. It was for me a haunted room I dared

41

not visit, with mice and cockroaches no doubt swarming between unpainted walls. I had seen once through the open door a naked light-bulb hanging in the centre.

Already he was putting on his clothes. I thought of him in that dark room, and of myself in this room, also alone. As he pulled on his trousers, I changed my mind. We had begun our secret rebellion. Having broken the first unjust law, we might as well go on and break the rest, especially if in breaking them we pleased ourselves. For, besides, I did not want him to go. I did not fear being alone – only, I no longer wanted to be.

'You really oughtn't to, you know. But I don't see *why* you shouldn't stay. After all, nobody need know. You can go at five or six, before the house is up. Nobody will know.'

'Nobody will know,' he whispered. Immediately he undressed again. He climbed back into bed and hugged me with his whole warm body. And then, in a few moments, he was asleep. I soon followed.

At five he went, hardly waking me, and managed to replace the screen from the outside. At seven thirty, when Nana knocked to wake me, I heard him mowing the lawn.

On weekdays after that he came each evening, bathed, and we studied and slept. He rose promptly at five, departing so quietly that I seldom heard him go at all.

VIII.

Our classes continued for four years. In that time, Chayo grew more rapidly than I, always stronger and more impetuous. I wore my glasses now all the time and had the look of one who was born with them. Against Chayo's physical energy I could only match one quality of my own: a wilful earnestness. In a teacher it was a useful quality. Whatever I learned at school I relayed to my pupil, usually in an embroidered form, and he received it intelligently. He kept little notebooks, as much to please me as himself; and there were other books I'd bought him with my own pocket money or out of his meagre wages. But there was a two-way traffic between us. Many nights he would bring small treasures from the garden, peculiar feathers or spiders or flowers. Once in a jar he brought a pale scorpion covered by her clinging offspring – a multitude of tiny scorpions, fixed to her like lice. He took the jar away with him and buried it. If he had nothing to show me, he would explain his new plantings, the rains, or whatever crucial events the garden waited for or had survived. And we considered the extra-curricular questions which puzzle boys of that age. The scope of our speculations was cosmic and comfortably undirected.

I made no friends at school. My difficulty with speaking the English language fluently set me apart as a quiet boy, and my extrovert schoolmates had no patience with 'the stammerer'. They were jealous, too, of my good results, for despite my difficulty in speaking English, I could write a dry, accurate prose. Chayo, of course, had no opportunity of making acquaintances on the green island, remote from San Jacinto except on Sundays, when he was in the tow of Doña Constanza and in the cathedral – hardly a place for striking up friendships. Nor did he – unusually for a native – have relations to go to. Nana had cousins in every corner of her *tierra*. But Chayo had only a missing father and a missing mother.

Isolated together there, we were as a result virtual brothers. But our intimacy, which had been public to begin with and had pleased my parents, was now secret. Even Nana seemed to take it for granted that we were little more now than boss and workman. She even suggested that I might prefer it if Chayo no longer joined us for meals in the pantry. I insisted he should stay. But by day, because of our evening meetings, we could afford to seem distant with one another, apart from the occasional skirmishes on the lawn or explorations along the river. My father's interdiction had turned ours into a furtive brotherhood.

The weekends, when my parents were in residence, were at first times of exile for Chayo. To get over this injustice, I took our conspiracy one step further. I decided that on such occasions it was my duty to join *him* in the gardener's shack near the gate.

On those weekend evenings we did not pursue our amorphous curriculum. Instead, we lay in his room on the narrow bed that sagged like a thick hammock beneath us. There he had slept first with his drunken father (except when he had pushed the boy off to sleep on the concrete floor), and later alone. We reflected on possible improvements to the place when I should become the owner of the green island. Like many rich children, I shared out my inheritance while the man who accumulated the fortune slept soundly in a room nearby. We plotted fantastic adventures – forays into San Jacinto, night expeditions to the river. One night we went down through the garden – grown unfamiliar and haunted in the dark, with trailing spider threads and sudden noises in the foliage – to the water.

To begin with, it was a terror to visit him in his shack. My parents' presence in the house rendered the exploit more dangerous and savoury, for by now it was an acute form of pleasure to break the arbitrary laws with which my father controlled the green island. Removing the screen, I would climb down the vines and creep along through the deep jasmine shrubs, keeping well in to the house so that, if either of my parents was at the window taking the air, they would not spy me. The spiders provided the greatest terror. Their unexpected nets snared my face and hands. By daylight, the actual creatures were bad enough, but at night imagination doubled them in size and virulence. Having got past the house, I crept along the lower wall by the oleander hedge, then up two disused steps to the rutted drive. I had first established the route by daylight, removing stones and other obstacles to have a clear run.

I tapped on Chayo's door. The place had lost its forbidding aspect. It was now merely a damp, shabby outpost from which to rescue my friend whenever I could.

When he heard me, he put out the light. The wooden door opened invisibly and his hand found mine and led me down the two steps into the room's utter dark. I found my way to the bed while he closed the door. Then he joined me there. We would lie in the dark and talk. It is strange that I never saw his room in full daylight at this time, nor he mine.

I woke less easily than he, and less punctually. At five it was his task to put me out. He would roll me over on my back and pick my glasses up off the floor, placing them on my face. Then he would jab me in the ribs. 'You're like Nana, putting out the cat,' I said irritably; or 'You're not very hospitable.' Then I stumbled to my feet and had the night-mare journey back along the walls, under the windows, and up into my room. Chayo always accompanied me to the edge of the house.

My parents never missed me, never called me in the evening from my room, or – looking to see if I was comfortable – discovered the door was locked. On Sunday, before sunrise, returning to my room, I would wind my clock and climb into bed, sleep an hour or two, and then be wakened by my father's loud knock. 'Time for church!' he shouted in the hall. And because of the lack of sleep the night before, I always felt 'delicate' on Sundays. My mother found me sullen and unresponsive.

IX.

My parents took me, out of courtesy, to the Reverend Purse's
Sunday service. They took Nana and Chayo in the car too,
but deposited them at the great cathedral gates. I envied
them, for the cathedral, with its high dome, and the censers
and processions, the large well-dressed plaster saints, the
guttering candles and the votive hearts, the women in black
with their lace veils and the men stolidly mumbling the
responses, – the cathedral was paradise itself beside the Reverend Purse's stark, saintless, ill-swept meeting-house. And
the Latin sounded more magical than the mere English of the
Episcopal service. When Nana took me to church with her as
a special treat on festivals that fell during the week, I knelt
gladly with her and even made prayers to her attentive saints.
But in the Reverend Purse's church I squatted like my parents
on the pews. I did not sing. I did not pray. The silver peso
I was given to put in the collection bag I put in grudgingly.
It was a tax demanded, not an act of voluntary charity. As
I grew older, I refused even to squat out of respect for the
other worshippers, but instead sat upright, staring blandly at
the Reverend Purse.

It was when he noticed this insubordination on my part
that he suggested to my mother that the time had come for
my spirit to be prepared for Confirmation. 'He seems to need
a little instruction in how the service works,' he said politely,
diplomatically – for she too had noted my refusal to bow to
the rubrics. It was hardly seemly, she thought, in the son of
a man in my father's position. I was wilful and marred the
general harmony.

The faces of my schoolmates were scattered among the
larger, saggy faces of their parents. Much of the expatriate
community attended the Reverend Purse's church – if not
each Sunday, at least on an unsystematic rota, so that there
was always a good showing, and more turned up afterwards
for the 'social' in the vestry – cold coffee, lemonade, and loud
conversation. It embarrassed me, it stiffened me to be there.
I could not speak as my schoolmates did. So I kept silent,

hid my accent and my stammer. Surveying them during prayer (I dared not do so during the sermons, when I put my best face of attention on) I felt an interloper among them. I could not understand what they were after in bowing their heads under so much sanctimonious language from the Reverend Purse. It was a spiritless service in a drab church, with a faded rector. There was no magic, no agreement even in the way they prayed.

I described these people to Chayo. 'I don't belong with them at all. I belong with Nana and you, at the cathedral, where they know what they're doing.' But Chayo shook his head.

'You may *want* to go to the cathedral with us. But wanting to go isn't belonging. It's not choice,' he said.

Until we were fourteen, I had not reflected that any difference existed between us. And certainly, whenever I said to Nana that I was one of her people (and she always called me her *hijo*, her son, in such a way that I could have believed her) she never disagreed. But my scholar, my brother Chayo, felt differently. Of course I knew that in the eyes of the world we were different – socially. He was the gardener and I the son of a wealthy businessman. But if I had the authority of the nominal 'patroncito', the little master, I did not exert it. And Chayo had the physical authority, being stronger than I, as he proved whenever we fought. I might be the 'professor', but he kept pace with me, and he had the garden as a province of primary experience far richer than my own acquired knowledge. We spoke the same language with the same accent. That he could not speak English put no distance between us. He never asked to, and besides, it was a language I used only on sufferance.

Chayo saw more clearly than I could the directions our increasing differences would take. For when I asserted – as though assertion could make it true – that I belonged with Nana and with him, he grew silent. And when I sullenly challenged him to speak up, he did so only reluctantly, as though it hurt him, and as though he was not quite certain, but felt he understood. We were fourteen. The world was less simple than it had been.

When we were in his dark room on weekends, with the sporadic assault of mosquitoes upon us, and I pressed him to

47

talk, he would begin simply. 'You do not live in this sort of place' – as though that were sufficient explanation.

'Not all your people live like this, you know. It has nothing to do with wealth.'

'It has *something* to do with wealth.' And he took the battery torch from my hand, beaming it up into his face. 'There is also the fact that we have different blood.' I could not argue with that. I no longer spent so much time with him out of doors. My skin was pale. He beamed the light in my face and with his other hand tugged at my hair. 'And that.' These were accidents. But to him they were evidence of more substantial problems. He belonged among them by nature – though he had no relation among them, no friends, no connections. I could only be one of them by effort, and never wholly, never unchallenged, but always having to prove my right. A place among them, but not of them. . . Born in their country, but with the wrong blood in my veins. . . Like a cuckoo in a borrowed nest. It seemed easy enough then, because I willed it passionately, for the cuckoo to become a sparrow. It certainly did not wish to follow its nature and become a cuckoo. I did not wish to be like my schoolmates. Any world I had been offered in exchange for the one Nana had built around me, and Chayo shared with me, would have seemed – even had it promised travel to the ends of the earth – inadequate. At the age of fourteen, I had spent most of the life I could remember in that house, among those people, never bored even when I was most ill. Though the money which sustained us came from my father, we did not live here simply by virtue of his money or his will. They may have brought us together in the first place, but they did not determine our compatibility, the patterns of life we evolved in his absence, nor the degree of our happiness. We were, to some extent, free to go. Should the wages cease, Chayo and I, Nana and I, could somehow manage elsewhere, having created a coherence in this place. It seemed blindingly clear.

But not to Chayo. He grew almost involuntarily more aware of my position, my family, my blood. He would call me 'boss' and rile me. He foresaw distinct futures for us, as though we had no will of our own in determining them, and our life together counted for nothing in the inexorable pattern of social division. He irritated me with his insistence, and as he grew more convinced, so I grew more emphatic and earnest

48

in my protestations to the contrary. I lavished my inheritance upon him, I gave him the metaphorical keys to the vineyard. I promised him so much, and so urgently, that at last he laughed at me. Our arguments ended in fights, but fights not without an element of anger. What most rankled with me was his passive acceptance of things as he saw them, as though that was the way it was, and we were moving down courses so well worn that no detour, no change of direction was permitted. He did not say, 'Prove you are one of us,' but merely, 'It is impossible for you to be one of us.' There was no challenge he could offer me. But as far as I was concerned, I had a choice, and I wanted to make it – but I could not unless he believed it existed too.

It was only later that I realized the real difference. I had a choice, maybe. But he had none. I did not teach him English. I had not given him the opportunity I chose for myself. It never struck me that he might wish to travel in the other direction. I doubt that he would have, but he did not get the chance.

One night he asked me, 'Is your father buying up more land?'

'Yes.' He planned to annex two further fields to the garden.

'Last time he bought land it was to extend the orchard. That's when my father came.'

'This time he plans another, bigger orchard.'

'Where is the first?'

'It's in his mind,' I laughed. But he was serious.

'He imagines his garden spreading and spreading, until it takes in all the dead fields around here.'

'It's a nice idea, don't you think?'

'If he gets another gardener.'

'You don't like the idea?' I asked anxiously.

'Do you imagine, like he does, the garden spreading and spreading?'

'I don't see why not,' I said. It was an agreeable image my father had. 'You've done it with this hillside, made it a proper little Eden. Think of all the dry land becoming garden and orchard, spreading out like moss on stone.'

'But the opposite will be true,' said Chayo quietly. 'The garden is bound to shrink.' I thought he had in mind the labour of keeping the watered wilderness in garden form, forcing the rare flowers and fruit to grow against the current of the climate and the hunger of the insects, destroying the thistles that leapt the fence and grew with appalling speed among the vegetables and in the shrubbery. And there was the long dry season, the surrounding fields parched, the nearby peasants living from week to week while we ate comfortably in the pantry. 'The garden is temporary,' said Chayo, scratching his stomach thoughtfully. 'I don't know what it's for. I keep it up. But no one really appreciates it. I mean, even you don't spend much time in it any more. Your mother and father come two days a week and walk around it once, complaining if they find weeds in the flower-beds. But what does it mean to them? A few vegetables get to their table, but more grow than they can ever eat, and the things that are left over get wasted. They don't need it. They don't use it.' He spoke musingly, not with anger, but incomprehension. 'You imagine the garden spreading to take in the yellow fields. You agree with your father. But look at the fields, and then look at the garden. The fields go on for miles, the green island is lost in them. It is a battle to keep it here, but the fields are not that sort of battle. When the rains come, they sprout, and if the weather is good, a small harvest is taken. The rest of the year they lie there and the scorpions live in them. It's natural. But the garden is not natural. It is something made which will not stay but needs to be made over and over again.'

'It's natural in another sense.'

'I don't understand you.'

I could not explain then. I knew, though, that my pupil was travelling a road down which I could not follow him. We talked no more of it that evening, but it surfaced with increasing frequency in later months, until it became a regular source of contention. 'I want to understand what you mean,' I would say. But more than that, I wanted to be as he was, think as he did, go to the cathedral with him and Nana, to have a job that absorbed me as his garden absorbed him, to be strong and equal to him in our fights. I wanted not to be alien to him, despite complexion, education, parentage; to persuade him that these counted for nothing if one willed them away. I wanted to make the choice.

X.

My favourite of Nana's religious feasts was the feast of San Isidro, patron of farmers and gardeners. Every new year I consulted the calendar to see if it fell on a weekday, which meant Nana would let me accompany her to his church, out of sight of my parents' deity. San Isidro was among Nana's favourite saints ever since he 'ended the great drought for me', as she put it. He did it only after considerable bidding, but she gave him credit and paid him several candles and votive tokens every year.

His was a sturdy white colonial church, conveniently on our side of town. A grey stone tracery decorated its white-washed face, and it was crowned with a belfry and tower tiled with blue and white Talavera from Puebla. The bells no longer sounded. Instead, the tower was equipped with loud speakers to broadcast a recorded peal of bells. A neon cross that flickered red by day and night, like a stray nerve, completed the tower. It was the only important old building in the 'low town' or 'new town'.

The church was set back in a large yard, and there the *feria* of San Isidro was staged. But because Nana took me to the four o'clock service, just after school, and the *feria* did not begin until seven in the evening, I had not seen the rides in action. The dead afternoon fairground was like a prehistoric boneyard, drab beside the sunlit church. It was a night world which daylight reduced to metal and chipped paint from fantasy. A flimsy rope excluded the public until it was time to celebrate on the big wheel, or the carousel, or in the shooting alleys. I was more fascinated by the church than by the 'machines of torment', as Nana called them. 'They are unsafe. Look at that rust!' she exclaimed, with a gesture which included not only the machines but those who made them turn and those who rode upon them.

In my fourteenth year, the feast of San Isidro fell on a Tuesday. The Reverend Purse had already begun paying me his Thursday attentions. It was a particular pleasure to rebel against his sensible, narrow teaching ('all this idolatry', as he

51

called the great feasts of the saints) and to walk arm in arm with Nana (I was now taller than she) along the avenue of tulipanes that shaded the way to the church door. We were part of a tide of worshippers pressing towards the dark entrance. Each of them, no doubt, claimed an intimacy like Nana's with the saint – farmers; aged women, with sticks, wearing long black veils; women with children; schoolboys. Surely, I thought, conducting an imaginary discussion with Chayo, among this variety of features and postures, the expressions of the faithful, there was a place for me, blond though I was, bespectacled, with all my other disabilities. I would demand from him a place in this diversity.

Nana reminded me that we received an indulgence just by crossing the threshold of the church. There was a plaque above the door to confirm this, and collection boxes flanked the entrance like sentinels who insisted on being acknowledged. She dropped fifty centavos into one of them, then genuflected towards the altar. I did likewise, gazing along the nave to the golden reredos. The atmosphere was thick with the scent of lilies, humanity and stale incense. We purchased two of the tubby little *veladoras* or devotional candles and joined the crowd at the chapel of San Isidro. From the foot of the saint's pedestal extended a bank of candles, as if flickering flowers crowding round their patron. Their light caught the gold-leaf fleurs-de-lis in the saint's carved wooden skirt. He seemed to burn quietly with the offerings, but his face gazed upwards. He ignored us, and the little flames. The eyes shone like the marble eyes of a stuffed animal, and you might read into them any passion you liked. Nana and I lit our *veladoras* at the large candle, when our turn came.

Then we made our way along the side of the church to a crowded pew and squeezed ourselves onto the end, just within sight of the main altar. The wall to my right was covered with an ancient battered fresco representing the miracle of the loaves and fishes. It must have been the work of a native artist, for the ship that brought Christ, moored in the uphill harbour, looked far from seaworthy – more the work of a man who has heard about ships, than a man who has travelled to the new world in one. The faces that gazed towards Christ were Indian faces, and Christ himself had the good-natured expression of a host among friends. The scene lacked solemnity. The loaves were rough-baked and the fish had eyes with pupils in them and looked far from dead. In such a scene the worshippers might see themselves in company with Christ. For the artist in including his contemporaries three hundred years ago had included their descendants as well. There was Nana's face – though cured of her white eye – plump and attentive, a little stiffly rendered, perhaps, but almost smiling. There, a young fisherman with broad lips, seriously studying the face of Christ. That was Chayo. Had I lingered I could have placed each of those who prayed with us that day at the feast in the native artist's parable. How inclusive he had been! Only, I did not see myself.

Nana interrupted my reflections. She nudged me. The service had begun. And the worshippers were in earnest. The prayers knocked hard at the ear, alms jingled into the collection bags. I showed Nana three silver pesos before I dropped them in. She squeezed my hand. The service kept us busy, bobbing up and down, crossing ourselves and genuflecting in the cramped space. I had not been to church with Nana frequently enough to follow the service. So I followed her.

It was a particular treat to watch her pray to San Martin, whose image occupied a pedestal some five yards in front of us. She looked at him as she might at a holy man. He was distant from her only a little, a slightly super-human authority who had it in his power to do some favour if she asked him in the right way. She moved her lips as she prayed, like a person reading; the lines around the mouth pursed and released, small sounds emerged – stray sibilants, the clicking of the tongue, but no audible word; the faint moustache on her upper lip trembled. She gazed upward at the saint's face, then deferentially down, then back again, her hands clutching and unclutching before her in small gesticulations such as she used in conversation. And she was in conversation. There was no human distance between her and her saint.

When the service was over, we did not leave the church immediately but made our way through the press of people to visit every saint and pay our respects, however briefly. Nana was a familiar face to the other parishioners. They may have known her for her cures, since she had become a little famous for them. They had probably seen her at the market, where she went twice a week for provisions. In any event, they greeted her as we passed, and as we emerged into the sharp sunlight, they nodded to her and gazed at me as well.

Some of them knew that she worked on the green island, tending a sick gringo child. This must be her charge. And they included me in their greeting, half-familiarly. We passed along the avenue of tulipanes to the gate of the church in silence, Nana nodding back to those she recognized, winking her white eye now and again.

She always rewarded my good behaviour at church with a special dinner. I walked beside her happy with expectation, and pleased to be in her company. How different hers was from my parents' church. Here you could pray to a manifest saint, a visibly human Virgin Mary, a crucified Christ that seemed to breathe forgiveness through his agony. In the Reverend Purse's church we knelt or squatted, gazed at our hands, into the air, or at our feet. Or else we focused on the rector himself. Apart from the plain wooden cross, there was no image to rivet our devotions. One felt only a pervasive absence, as though the God we invoked lived in a distant country.

The congregation here did not linger for coffee and conversation in the vestry. Some hurried back to work, others went home. A few, up from the country, made their way to the bars in the upper town. Some sat down in the churchyard to wait in the cooling afternoon for the *feria* to open. It was only two hours off.

'You are an angel,' Nana said.

'San Isidro is the best of all the saints. I wish his day was always Tuesday.'

'No, son – all the saints are good. No saint is better than another.' She insisted on the point. 'You may have your favourites, but you mustn't say they're better. It might give offence.'

Equal saints – only the Virgin and perhaps Saint John had a little something extra.

We passed out through the church gate and into the dusty street. It was one of the few straight streets in the lower town, and not very long – ten blocks in each direction. At one end it petered out in a track that led into the fields. That way was downhill, and it seemed to drain the dusty, faded town into the yellow nullity that extended to the distant hills. In the other direction rose the sudden cliffs, and above them the old town continued. The cliffs were not more than forty feet high, but they were steep and ragged. Single boulders and outcrops were painted with election slogans and political messages, lawful graffiti in flaked red, white and green. On the cliff-top, where the straight street suddenly forked into two steep ascents, stood an older and far grander church than San Isidro's. It was grey now and derelict. It had not been reopened after the Revolution forty years before but stood there still, imposing and perilous. The mayor wanted to demolish it: the land it stood on was desirable real-estate. The state governor wanted to restore it as a museum of the Revolution. It waited their decision, occasionally releasing masonry, tiles or larger stones down the cliff-side, as if to remind the authorities that it was patient, but there was an end to patience. Nana told me the dome was on the verge of subsiding into the empty nave. 'We must pray that it does not fall. It will be restored.' And among her other prayers, Nana remembered the derelict church, which did not fall, despite the rumours and the flaking masonry.

XI.

That night over dinner I told Chayo about the service. In passing I mentioned the *feria*. His eyes darkened and he became tense and silent. Clearly he had some mischief in his mind. He ate rapidly, and whenever Nana's back was turned winked and gestured at me to hurry too. I took my time, however. I was receiving my reward for virtue and good behaviour, and San Isidro was being celebrated. I didn't intend to squander what I'd earned with so much pleasure. Chayo excused himself early and disappeared into the night.

After Nana's devotions I went to my room. I closed and locked the door. Before I could turn on the light a hand closed over my mouth. I tried to cry out. But I didn't struggle for long. It was Chayo. 'Hush! You'll bring Doña Constanza in on us and all will be lost!' He had removed the screen and entered – 'before your time,' I said, gasping with surprise – and in his impatience waited for me like a burglar in the dark.

'What *are* you up to?' I asked when he released me.

'We are going to the *feria!*'

This announcement struck me dumb for a moment. 'We can't go to the *feria*. It's too late.'

'It will be open beyond midnight.'

'But it's miles away. Nana and I had to come back by taxi.'

'Are you scared?'

'No.' And then, 'Yes.'

'But why? What of? We'll be together.'

'We might get robbed, or beaten up. Or someone will recognize me. Besides, I have to go to school in the morning. And what if Nana should find out?'

'No one need know.'

'You keep telling me how different I am from you. I'd stick out like a sore thumb at the *feria*.'

'We can take care of that. You can wear a disguise. Yes – you can put on my garden clothes and my hat. They'll not be able to tell you from anyone else. You'll be just another *peon*.'

'Do you think so?' I asked dubiously. And then, emphatically: 'I can't go.'

'Coward.'

'You go if you like.' But as I spoke, I knew that if he went I had to go too. I should be miserable if he went without me – there or anywhere else.

'Why do we keep planning excursions and never make them?' he demanded angrily. 'Here's a perfect adventure, and you immediately get cold feet. I'll go without you then, and I won't tell you one thing about it. I'll go have a good time by myself.'

'How will you get there?'

'Walk.'

'It'll take an hour and more.'

'I'll run, then.'

'There are dogs, though, all along the way.'

'They only bark. I know how to manage them.'

'What will you use for money?'

'I have money.'

'If I'd known you might go, I wouldn't have told you.'

He made his way to the window and removed the screen. 'Are you coming?'

'I'm coming.'

We went out through the window together into the cool night air and made our way to the gardener's shack. There we exchanged clothes. His trousers were still damp from his work in the garden, and his shirt with the sweat of the afternoon. I pulled his straw hat low on my head and bent the brim down to help conceal my glasses. I wore my own shoes, but otherwise I was entirely disguised as Chayo. He wore my clothes which – though a little small for him – suited him: the grey trousers and blue shirt. I'd never seen him so properly dressed.

We climbed over the front wall and stumbled up the dark track to the road. The exhilaration of wearing Chayo's clothes, of being him for a few hours and carrying his smell on my body, had overcome my reluctance for the adventure – as though his poor things communicated some charm. I tried to imitate his walk.

The dogs in the scattered neighbourhood barked from the four points of the compass. There was no moon, and the rutted track made the going hard. With his hat pulled low on my brow, I allowed myself to swear each time I tripped in one of the potholes. Nana would hardly have recognized her 'angel' of five hours earlier. Unlike me, Chayo was not relishing the journey, but rather the prospect of the *feria*.

'You look like a real *peon*,' he said to please me, 'when your face and hair are covered up.'

'Or in the dark.'

'We should have done this long ago,' he exclaimed jauntily, then tripped in a rut and fell vociferously onto his knees. I pulled him to his feet and brushed him down.

'Mind you don't tear my trousers.'

'You can do what you like with mine. I don't mind,' he said. Sooner than I expected, we saw a diffuse cloud of light ahead of us, and when we were over a mile away the sounds of the *feria* reached us – a mixture of music, the shriek of metal on metal, and the cries of people on the 'machines of torment'. We entered town between the dark houses, to the closer barking of watch-dogs. I expected gates to open, or the police to stop us. 'But the police,' said Chayo, 'will be at the *feria*, or drunk in bed, or with the whores. It's San Isidro's day, don't forget.'

We turned left into the street where the church stood, and then right into the churchyard. The scene was transformed from the afternoon. The red neon cross still flickered above the church, but against the other lights it was wan. The church itself seemed to have disappeared, replaced by a riot of coloured lights in the churchyard. Its portal was dark. The flimsy rope that had kept the worshippers from the *feria* that afternoon had been moved, so that the church was out of bounds now to the fair-goers. Entering the gate to the churchyard, one was compelled to enter the *feria*. Half the town seemed to have come.

'Those rides are unsafe,' I said, remembering the rust Nana had indicated earlier in the day. 'You don't want to risk your life on that!' He stood in the queue for the big wheel. In the cool night air, I began to perspire with fear. Chayo eyed the rickety steel circle.

'Shut up, *peon*. I'm the boss tonight. You're coming with me.' He took my arm firmly and led me to one of the hanging seats. It was a very old model, and one's feet dangled in the air. The sensation was like riding into the sky on a park bench, with only a thin leather strap securing you. Chayo paid for both of us, and a boy with a long scar from his ear down to his bare chest leaned across to strap us in. He glanced up at my face.

'He's a gringo, is he?' he asked Chayo.

'I'm not a gringo,' I said loudly – too loudly. The couple in the swing ahead of ours pivoted their heads and observed us. I shrank deep into Chayo's clothes. The wheel began to turn. We rose and fell, with an appalling grating sound above the raucous music. With my eyes closed, I despatched fervent prayers to San Isidro. His upward, marble gaze in the darkened church – perhaps we passed, again and again, through his field of vision. Perhaps he would remember the three pesos I had placed in his collection. Chayo, meanwhile, kept nudging me and pointing out the sights. He made a mental map of the rides we had to go on. When the first ordeal was over, the evening had only just begun.

We went from one ride to another until at last we reached the 'octopus'. Seated in the car of that infernal machine, and already nauseous with fright, I was flung against Chayo. I nearly despaired of San Isidro. 'Let yourself go!' Chayo shouted in my ear. When the music ceased, and the machine had given us our fifty centavos' worth, I opened my eyes to find I was clutching Chayo by the hand for safety. He grinned at me in the flickering light and seemed among the other faces distant, alien – not my pupil, at that moment not even my friend. 'Pull down your hat. Your face is showing,' he said, removing his hand from mine and playfully pulling at the brim of the hat I wore. Shakily I followed him towards the shooting alleys.

The worst terrors of the place were past, and so was most of Chayo's money. We wandered up and down the *feria* observing the people. In the unreal light they were all dream creatures. They were not like the characters in the mural of the loaves and fishes, nor the crowd that had stood aside to let Nana and me pass by that afternoon. I recognized only one face – that of the man who sold ices outside the school gate. He was there with his cart. I managed to avoid him. My schoolmates called him 'Typhoid' and bought his ices with a devil-may-care nonchalance. I never tasted them. His dirty white jacket repelled me, and especially the oiled moustache which he twisted at continually.

Chayo decided to spend his last coins at the shooting alley. All the air-rifles had slightly bent barrels so no one could win the larger prizes (moth-eaten dolls, bottles of liqueur). The attendant handed Chayo a rifle. 'And one for your little gringo friend?' she asked, winking at me. 'Doesn't he want to shoot?' I hurried off, while Chayo laughed and joked with the attendant. I pulled the brim of the hat down so smartly that I almost tore it. I wanted to disappear, or to reassume my own clothes and walk about boldly in my proper costume. Chayo followed me a few moments later. He put his arm round my shoulder.

'In the dark, you look like a *peon*. But even my clothes won't deceive them when they can see you. Don't worry about it. And look!' He held up before my eyes a small glass fish. 'A present for Doña Constanza. I won it at the shooting alley. Bang, bang, bang. Three down.'

'Where will you tell her you got it?'

'I'll tell her I found it. By the river. She'll take it for a miracle.' And she did. The one way to deceive Nana was through her faith.

San Isidro's own bells never sounded now. But the cathedral bells tolled midnight from the upper town, and we started back. The adventure was finished. Chayo talked about it in whispers all the way home. He was in love, he declared, with the girl who collected the money for the 'octopus'. 'If only it were on tomorrow too, I'd be back there.' He did not say 'alone', but I thought I heard the word.

It took us only three quarters of an hour to get to the gate again, and over, now we knew the route. We were back in Chayo's room. I took off his clothing. 'I really smell like you now,' I said, sniffing my arms and chest.

'We traded more than clothes, then! But you didn't fool anybody. Did you enjoy the adventure?'

'Yes and no.'

'Yes and no. Why do you talk like that?' He imitated my hesitancy, then prodded me in the ribs. 'You either did or you didn't. Say yes, because we know how to get to town now, and we'll be going again. You'll see.'

'Come back to my room.'

'It's too late for a class.'

'Come back anyway.' I took him by the hand and we went back through the night that seemed – despite the drone of insects – peaceful, almost silent, to the place where our adventure had begun. My head throbbed from the noise of the fairground. I drew Chayo along, aware of nothing so much as of his strangeness. I felt I must keep an eye on him. The trivial experience had altered him, filled him with a new excitement. He had taken some form of initiative from me. He had the upper hand.

Certainly, from that time, our discussions easily turned to arguments, and our arguments were heated. We were unable to control the note of acrimony that sometimes came into even the most trivial exchange. And Chayo began to create imaginary romances – the 'octopus' girl was the first – and demand that I believe in them. He spent a long time in front of my mirror, trying on my shirts and jackets, studying his face and arranging his expression to suit a series of fancied circumstances. He was well-favoured, but his vanity as it increased brought a note of strain into his naturally frank face, a sense of tension.

Out of my wardrobe I gave him whatever he wanted. Each gift he took with a rebuff. 'If your father paid me proper wages, a man's wages, I wouldn't have to beg these things from you.'

'It's not begging. What's mine is yours. You know that.' But there was enough justice in his accusation to irritate me, and my automatic response he could no longer credit. I felt like saying, 'Put me to the test.' But I restrained myself, for fear he would.

He was learning to handle me. And as the distance between us increased inevitably, I let myself be used, in the attempt to preserve what we had ceased to call our 'brotherhood'. When he suggested an adventure, I no longer hesitated. I assumed a fake enthusiasm. I put on his clothes again and again like an actor preparing for a role in which he has already failed, and knows he is about to fail again, and yet still cannot help feeling hope that this time it will go right. When he admired some item in my wardrobe, I made him accept it. At first he was bewildered by my new, automatic acquiescence. He distrusted it. It was some time before he came to take advantage of it. To begin with it was merely a pattern that became established, so that I followed where he wanted to go, but as soon as I knew the direction, I would pretend to lead the way.

And, despite the change that was occurring between us, there were many evenings when nothing went amiss, when I

was happy, we continued our studies and slept soundly in
one bed.

XII.

We made our furtive way to town often – as Chayo had determined we should. In the end we took to going, as by plan, once a week, on Tuesdays, so that I dreaded Wednesdays and the long Latin class at school through which I tried not to doze, the reprimands I got for sloth and carelessness. The rewards of our nocturnal expeditions were not much to boast of: we did not coincide with any of the other holy *ferias*. We came to know our way around various neighbourhoods, but not the neighbourhoods themselves, except their dogs – husky invisible dogs that bayed at us from behind the garden walls of the larger houses, and unchained mongrels that guarded the poorer areas. We became skilful in avoiding night-watchmen. I took Chayo past the Reverend Purse's dowdy church and past my school. We prowled around the state college in its lonely site between San Jacinto and the green island. Our adventures bored us, but we kept going – Chayo in search of drama or romance, and I – without expectations – in order not to lose sight of my friend. We stalked up the rutted track usually around eleven o'clock, and stumbled home again some time after two in the morning.

Only one of these later excursions stands out in my memory. In fact, it remains among my most vivid recollections. It was our most ambitious foray, taking us all the way across San Jacinto, from the lower town through the old upper town and beyond, where the poorest neighbourhood stretches into the hills. At the heart of this poor area stands the bold, square penitentiary, illuminated at night with arc lights and surrounded by a high stone wall surmounted with strands of barbed wire and an edge of glittering broken glass. The penitentiary was built well above the town, but like a magnet it drew into its shadow a colony of poverty and now overlooked the darkest neighbourhood.

We had tried to find the way to it before. But every earlier time we had chosen the wrong routes or entered long cul-de-sacs. That night, winding our way upward through the unpaved, reeking streets of what Nana (who had never been there) referred to as 'the lost city on the hill', we had almost decided to turn back when, rounding a corner, we saw the penitentiary rising before us, a large blind building skirted with a wide, empty unpaved area, and then the low shacks, the dives and bars began, facing the no-man's-land. Along the top of the penitentiary building we saw armed sentries pacing to and fro. A few policemen patrolled the civilian side of no-man's-land.

As we gazed up at the penitentiary, one of the near-side policemen spotted us. He called out to halt. 'Run!' Chayo whispered. We were near enough the mouth of the alley from which we had just emerged to flee back down it. We ran. The footsteps of the policeman sounded after us. We turned into another alleyway, another, until we had lost him. He was not persistent in his search. Had he wished to catch us, he could have followed the trail of frenzied, barking dogs we had aroused.

'We should have stopped and spoken to him,' I whispered.

'You're crazy. What would you have told him you were doing? Dressed as a *peon*, with your *gringo* face? He would have taken us inside and locked us up. He would have called Doña Constanza. And what would you tell her? Once they have you, it costs a lot to get out again.'

Certainly we were a suspicious pair. And in our estimation we were law-breakers: the penitentiary had some claim upon us. Even if we had not broken the laws of the land, we were not anxious to test the reasonableness and good will of the San Jacinto police force.

We had lost the policeman. But, as we caught our breath, we realized that we had lost our way as well. The penitentiary was out of sight. We found ourselves in an altogether strange alleyway, with one small high street-lamp whose glow was too weak to clarify the ground. This alley emptied into another. We were climbing higher into the poorest part of the lost town.

'I wish I had a stick for the dogs,' Chayo said. He was afraid. I felt a selfish sort of comfort, disguised in his clothes that made me seem more like a native of the place than he did wearing my attire. He was conspicuous and uncomfortable. We stopped at last in a dark corner to confer.

'Where are we?'

'This is the district of the whores.'

'What does that mean?'

'Whores.'

'I know what they are. But where are we?' He did not reply but led me the length of the alley to where it emptied into a wider thoroughfare, an ill-paved street, straight and steep. 'There! At the bottom of the street, the penitentiary!' I whispered. 'Now we can find our way back.' I was about to descend towards the known landmark when Chayo detained me.

'Wait, look up there.' He pointed to the right, a short way up the street. Over most of the doors were strings of fairy-lights, and in a few doorways sat solitary women on small chairs, their faces and dresses mottled by the illumination. On a corner opposite the swing doors of a bar called *Las Flores del Deseo* opened and closed, a naked blue bulb illuminating the fanciful sign in which each 'o' in the name was a painted daisy. The blue light seemed to chill the passers-by into ghosts; those who entered the bar or came away laughed and talked in loud voices raw with drink. As we watched, we formed some idea of the clientele of *Las Flores* – numerous and purposeful. People went in one by one and emerged in pairs. When the doors opened, we had brief glimpses into the smoky interior of the place.

Two women, arm in arm, climbed the street towards the bar. Their conversation was animated and harsh. They had almost passed our alley opening when, with a shriek, one of them spotted me. She laughed aloud when she saw what I was – not a lurking man but just a boy, a *peon*, to judge from my clothes. Chayo's hat was drawn low over my eyes. My disguise at last had fooled someone. 'Crawl back under your stone, you slinky bastard. What's the idea of scaring ladies to death?' They passed. They had not noticed Chayo who had withdrawn behind me. When they reached the bar, they divided and went in through different doors.

'Watch. They won't be in there for long,' said Chayo, 'and when they come out it's not arm in arm. They're whores,' he added, knowingly. We waited, observing the comings and goings. Chayo's prediction was correct. The women we were watching for emerged separately, each with a man on her arm. The couples left a discreet few paces between them. Again they crossed over and passed our alley opening, talking this time in different tones. They had taken up their roles and

65

softened their manner. They were too involved in the matter of pleasing their clients to notice us. We had drawn back further into shadow for fear of alarming them once more.

As soon as they had passed, I turned to Chayo to tell him the time. It was getting far too late for us. 'A little longer,' he said. 'Follow her, the second one.' She and her friend had just gone round the corner.

'What *for*?' I asked. But Chayo did not delay to answer. He took me by the wrist, drawing me out of hiding. We ran down close by the house-fronts and reached the alleyway she had taken, in time to see her disappear, with her friend, through a narrow passage between the houses.

'Come along!' I did not stop him but followed like a blind man finding his way by sound. If I lost Chayo in the maze of alleys, I doubted whether we should ever get home again. I could not rebel against his sudden plans for fear that he would decide to shake me off in the lost town.

At the end of the passage the woman and her client had entered, a thin light was visible. We reached a diminutive courtyard at the centre of five or six ramshackle dwellings. From one came the distorted sound of a transistor radio. We stood in shadows by a post that supported a sloping, tiled terrace roof. Tin cans with geranium plants lined one low wall, and an oil drum served as water-butt near the door. As we stood by a dark window, a light came on behind us, and we moved aside like curtains, one to either end of the window, afraid that we had been seen. But the woman and her friend were busy with each other. Casually she came to the window and drew the flimsy inner curtains together. They were ill-fitting, and when they joined at the centre, they left the sides uncovered.

The light within was one naked bulb, dangling from the ceiling of the room. Chayo at his side of the window and I at mine had a spectral vantage through and around the gauze curtain. The woman removed her shawl with a lazy flourish. She was large. Her blonde hair had not been retouched for some time and rose out of dark roots. The small man who had accompanied her was soon beside her, helping her to undress. For himself, he needed no assistance.

The sagging mattress they sat on had no covering. They carried out their brief transaction without ceremony. I closed my eyes. When I looked again, they had lain back on the

66

mattress, the woman keeping her large arm beneath her friend, to draw him back on to her when he was ready. From where I stood in the shadow, they appeared disfigured. Her large breasts hung either side of her chest. Her knees were drawn up. She cast enormous shadows. The little man was like a grasshopper on a huge vegetable, soon ready again. They began to repeat their business, this time more slowly.

'Chayo!' I whispered.

'In a moment.' I could see the light reflecting off his face, his eyes attentive to the scene. On hands and knees I crawled beneath the window and grabbed him by the ankle.

'We're going!' I had broken the spell. He looked away, dropped to his hands and knees, and crawled back with me. We ran down the passage, into the alleyway and back to the street.

'That was wrong,' I said, referring to our spying.

'It was natural,' he said, misunderstanding me. He grabbed my trousers at the crotch. 'See! You enjoyed it. And so did I,' he added, taking my hand and placing it on the swelling in his own trousers. I recoiled.

'We have to get home. It's after two.' And we ran, choosing the route to the penitentiary, and then any street which led down the hill, until we were at the cathedral. From there we knew the way.

This adventure satisfied Chayo. He talked about it merrily all the way home. 'But I'll be inside next time.'

'You won't catch me dead in there.'

'No doubt.' We exchanged clothes in his room. I was surprised to see he was still sexually excited. 'I'll come back with you,' he said hoarsely. He put his arm around me and pressed his body against mine.

'You stay here tonight,' I said, and left him in his room. I climbed into my own, replacing the screen and closing the window. I showered, but the smell of Chayo's clothes seemed to hang about me as I crawled into bed. There was no chance of sleep that night. The images would not disappear, nor the sensation of Chayo's body. My bed seemed large and empty. A strong disgust filled my throat like nausea. I had not slept alone for years.

XIII.

My catechism became a slow, deliberate, and I began to feel a deliberately endless affair. The rector enjoyed bouncing his little Hillman down the track to the green island, enjoyed the power he had of summoning – by means of his petulant, persistent little claxon – Chayo to open the gates and admit him. He relished the luxury of his whiskies on the verandah, watery though they were, and despite what he called his 'language difficulties' with 'that dear Doña Constanza, who *always* sends me iced tea when I arrive'. And he took evident, increasing pleasure in our classes, even as I came to resent them more and more. He eyed me with a repulsive, ingratiating approval that made it impossible for me to return or even meet the gaze of his dull, pink-rimmed eyes. I was too reticent to be uncivil, and I spoke as little as I could because my tongue stammered when I spoke English. But in moments of frustration, sometimes I would manage to articulate an awkward question. This delighted him. He would sit back and savour it and shape a reply or a retort, full of the satisfaction of having roused me, kindled my interest, and persuaded that I enjoyed his intellectual attention. He would reply, and if I was within reach, he would pat my hand. Occasionally he would get to his feet, walk about the verandah constructing sentences, and pat me on the head when he returned to his drink. 'When I wander round this charming verandah, talking with you, I know how Socrates felt.' He would digress into an evocation of that 'other teacher's' school.

Several months' labour took us little nearer to salvation. We had puzzled our way through a few clauses of the Creed. I heard much of the story of his life, his eternal disappointments. He gave me a diverse sampling from his repertoire of opinions and prejudices. Always unctuously benign, his broad sun-reddened pate pricked with sweat, he beamed at himself and invited my applause for each of his laborious *bon mots*, his clarifications, and what he liked to call his 'encapsulations' of points of dogma. In the end, I understood more or less *what* he believed, but not why – as though a man with an habitual tic in his left eye described the obvious physical aspect of it, without describing the sensation he experienced, or the cause he believed to lie behind it.

I grew accustomed to listening to him. I learned to take a spare sort of pleasure from his reading aloud – not least because it drew his attention away from me and onto a page of print. His voice was a good instrument when it performed the words of others. I came to regard the Episcopalian faith as his job rather than his vocation. He was a salesman.

I was unprepared one Thursday, when I arrived home at my usual, slightly late hour, to find a very different Reverend Purse on the verandah. He seemed to be chomping at his drink. Sweat twinkled on his crown and ran down his cheeks, the pale eyes had become darker, pursed in their lids. He did not rise to greet me with his customary, tiresome civility.

'Am I very late, sir?' I asked, glancing at my wrist-watch. I shook it to see if the hands had stopped.

'No more so than usual,' he replied curtly. 'Hurry up, boy. Stop gawking. Get your books together and let's get on with it.' I hastened to my room, more curious than apprehensive about the change that had come over him. The familiar rector had entirely disappeared.

Our class went jaggedly. He asked question after question, interrupting my replies. 'Speak up, boy. Must you always stammer? Don't they teach you how to speak properly at school?' He interjected sarcasms at my expense. His manner turned sharper and darker with each of my falterings. At last, having considered all possible causes for his anger I could think of, and being unable to blame myself on any count, I thought to bring the matter to a head. If I was guilty, he should point his finger at the fault. I would try to mend it if I could. If I was not guilty, then he should take his revenge on the cause, not on me as surrogate.

'Have I done something wrong, sir?' I asked so candidly and innocently that he came up short against it in his fury.

'No, you haven't. Now answer my question and get on with it. I asked you to recite the confession.'

'I only asked because you seem very agitated,' I said, ignoring the question.

'Damn your impertinence! Do as I say.'

I was learning the service by heart, week after week, rubric by rubric. My memory was porous. I was exhausted, too, with Chayo's and my expeditions, our classes, the school work. I started again to recite the confession, but the words got garbled. On the verandah in the warm afternoon, with an inexplicably uncivil catechist, I made several false starts. At last, despite his interruptions and sarcastic fulminations, I got half way through: 'there is no health in us. But'

'But what, boy?'

'I'm afraid I've forgotten again.'

'Stop. I can't take any more of this – this stupidity.' He lurched to his feet, after a mere half an hour, thrust his Panama hat onto his head, took his walking stick (in lighter moments, he called it his 'swagger stick') and made his way towards the front gate, where his little Hillman waited for him. 'Next Thursday. At four *sharp*. Make sure you get it right by then, boy.'

His rage seemed directed, as it were, over my shoulder. He didn't look at me, and yet his anger included me. He was so angry he had not even finished his cocktail.

'Wait!' I called after him. 'I'll have Chayo open the gate for you.'

'Chayo be damned!' he shouted. 'Send Doña Constanza. I can do without the indignity of seeing your little friend again. He can go to hell.' I sent Doña Constanza. So! Chayo was at the root of this.

I went to find him, to find out why the rector had taken so suddenly, absolutely, against my friend – my 'little friend' – about whom he had questioned me once with such warmth that I was tempted to disclose to him the extent of our friendship, our classes and fraternity. The rector's hostility was now so vehement that it made me apprehensive. I knew Chayo despised the man. He had been particularly bristly in recent days, aimlessly impatient, unsmiling.

I found him edging the lawn on the lower terrace. When I approached he grinned at me like a cat, mischievously savage. He moved along on his knees, skilfully managing the edging shears. The ignition cough and then the screech of tyres of the rector's Hillman – casting off from the green island in rage – further broadened Chayo's grin.

'What have you done to that man?'

'Nothing.'

'Come – you must have done something. He's bright red

and furious. He spent half an hour getting at me, then he swore and got up and went.'

'None of my business.'

'He said you should go to hell.'

'Maybe I can.' His face convulsed, then a large hoarse laugh escaped, and another, until he was guffawing uncontrolledly. Between storms of laughter he got the story out. The laughter was without merriment. It came from some part of him I had not encountered before – a mindless, hysterical part over which he exercised no control, which took him beyond me, beyond himself.

The rector, he said, wandering about as he awaited my arrival, had come upon Chayo in the upper garden where he was weeding one of the flower-beds. In the execrable Spanish of a lazy immigrant who has never made the effort – in fifteen years – to learn properly the language of the land, and yet who hasn't the tact to know his limitations, he had asked the boy whether his spiritual health was being attended to. Did he go to church and catechism?

'I have not even been to school, sir.'

The rector struggled to express to him that such a statement smacked of ingratitude to his employer, my father. He then emitted some broken sentences which Chayo could not follow but which were so amusingly garbled that Chayo laughed. Startled at this response, the Reverend Purse had put his hand on the boy's shoulder, earnestly looked him in the eye, and urged him to come to Episcopalian confirmation classes. Though the course was half-complete already, the rector promised Chayo private tuition, if he wished, at the rectory – 'in Spanish', he had added. The proposition was accompanied by a series of expressive pressures to his shoulder and arm.

'If that is Spanish, what language should I speak?' Chayo had asked – and then began to laugh hard in the rector's face. The earlier laughter Purse had read as good-natured, but this laughter was unmistakably insolent. He shook the boy by both shoulders hard, as a master might shake an insubordinate servant. Chayo was not a servant. He pushed the rector sharply off and – laughing still – gathered together his trowel and his basket of weeds and left the upper garden.

'But Chayo, he meant well,' I remonstrated.

'He did not mean well. He is an evil man.'

'Evil?'

'He likes my face,' he said, loading the four words with more venom than I could understand.

'That's a compliment.'

'Not from that man. Why me? Why doesn't he look to the souls of the urchins in the *mercado*, on his own doorstep?' His hilarity turned to an anger as deep and unexpected as the mirthless laughter that had shaken him. 'He thought it would be nice to impress your parents. "The gardener *peon* is going to be confirmed." '

'My father would have been furious.'

'He wasn't to know. And besides, I've seen him. The way he looks at me, the way he looks at you. I have eyes. He'd as soon have an arse as a soul. Private lessons! He's a hypocrite, using his privileges and the trust your father puts in him.'

'I don't understand you. Of course he's repulsive – we've always agreed about that. But, evil? He's just trying to be friendly.'

'You're very stupid, sometimes, Professor.' After his anger he was sullen. He was isolated with a knowledge he could not share with me because – though I understood what it was to feel guilt – I did not know what he meant by 'evil', a quality in other men.

He knelt on the grass clutching the edging shears. Then for the first time I had ever seen it, his eyes filled with tears. He struggled against them, but they welled up blinding him. He hurled down the shears. His face was contorted with a grief which changed him beyond recognition, for he could not stop fighting it, pulling his mouth tight, putting his fists to his eyes. He turned his back on me. He squatted on the lawn crying.

I put my hands on his shoulders. 'Stop it,' I said, feeling something in me being torn. He shook me off.

'Go away. You are stupid. You are like them.'

'Like whom?'

He didn't reply. He said, 'Go away now.' I moved away, leaving him there, pouring out a grief I had not known he had in him. He had not cried when his father ran off. He had never cried out of loneliness or fear in the months he slept alone. Why cry now, when someone asked after his spiritual welfare – a clumsy, trivial, insinuating someone, of no possible consequence? Why cry when someone liked his face? Looking

72

back at the huddled figure in the sweat- and grass-stained clothes, the shears lying angrily open on the lawn to his left, the fringe of clipped grass, and around the well-tended garden, the tamed wilderness on which he spent his life, that no one much noticed – and at the cracked straw hat that had fallen from his head and lay behind him, at his black hair mussed and dull with perspiration, at his forearms' dusty brown. . . I returned towards him. I put my hand on his arm. He looked up, his face drawn straight into a tight mask of control.

'It's over now,' he said and stood up trembling. 'It's over.' He leaned down to pick up the shears, replaced his hat on the back of his head, turned away from me and knelt again, mechanically continuing to trim the edge of the lawn.

XIV.

A week later, after catechism (the Reverend Purse had returned more or less to normal, as I expected he would, and made no allusion to the events of the previous week) – after catechism, after dinner and Nana's devotions, and after Chayo and I had conducted our class and were preparing for sleep, the world seemed back in joint, the pattern of our lives was re-established. After his laughter and tears the week before, Chayo was relaxed, exhausted, more apparently happy than he had been for months. A tension had been eased, but he did not speak of it. Each time I tried to press the conversation towards it, he sensed my direction and eluded me.

But it was Thursday night. My parents were coming tomorrow for the weekend. The Reverend Purse made his twice-monthly visit 'to report on your boy's progress' and to enjoy lunch and a few rubbers of bridge with my parents and their houseguests and – with tact and luck – to enjoy supper as well. He would be coming on Saturday. He might keep mum on the subject of Chayo's misconduct, thus preserving intact his 'dignity' where my parents were concerned. Or – as seemed more likely – he might tell them in some exaggerated form a tale which would redound to his credit and at the same time work some revenge on the helpless gardener, who had done nothing to solicit his attentions, and yet was to suffer as a result of them.

My father would have, in the latter case, to balance his indignation with the meddlesome rector, inviting the gardener to Episcopalian catechism ('the boy is native, and a Catholic, after all,' I could hear him say, straining between fury and the manner of civility) and his anger against Chayo for impoliteness to his betters. Chayo, I decided, would suffer more than the rector. My father was finding small faults with him already. His belief that however good the natives were to begin with, they always reverted to insolence and laziness, would be vindicated. Chayo would be made to conform to my father's 'law of nature'.

That Thursday night I was uneasy. I had to warn Chayo tactfully of what I feared, and I had to find out what his stance would be should my father reprimand him. In his early years he had loved and respected my father, counting him generous, grateful that he had not been sent to the orphanage. He asked me to talk about him. He responded with all the warmth of his childish nature to my father's cold civilities. But in recent months, niggling reprimands, complaints, the disdain with which my father dismissed his little plans for improvement of a flower bed, or planting a break of eucalyptus near the vegetable garden – plans which, earlier, my father would have approved casually, as of little consequence –; in short, the increasing, arbitrary use of the word 'no' by one who had encouraged Chayo's earlier initiatives, had cooled his affection and respect. He would ask me, 'In what way have I offended your father?' 'In nothing. He has told me nothing.' And like a man punished, without being told what crime he had committed, Chayo brooded. When he failed to turn up in his memory any cause for his disfavour, he began to distrust the affection he had felt for his master. And then, secretly, for he had not spoken of it to me, he began to dislike him.

Before Chayo settled down for sleep, I broached the question directly.

'The rector is coming to lunch on Saturday. I expect he will tell my father what happened last week.'

'So what?' said Chayo, yawning.

'You know how my father feels – about respect and that. . .'

'So long as it's respect for *him*,' Chayo said, and the bitterness came back into his voice.

'What do you mean?'

'He doesn't care much about other people's respect for me. He doesn't even care about my respect for myself.' He sat up abruptly. 'I'm fifteen now. He hasn't raised my salary once in all the time since my father left this place. I'm a man now. I need things. I can't always be begging from you.'

'You never *beg* from me. What's mine is yours, you know that.'

'That's just words.'

'No. I mean it. Whatever of mine you've wanted, I've lent to you or given it.'

'Give me your clock,' he said.

75

'But you don't *need* that.'

'It's need, then, is it? Give me all your clothes. Give me your books.'

'Now you're being absurd,' I said, trying to get the conversation back to the immediate problem. 'If he talks to my father, there may be trouble.'

'What sort of trouble?'

'My father likes you.'

'Not very much any more. He always complains – about nothing. He never lets me carry out any of my plans any more. I used to feel the garden was almost my own province, but not any more. As far as he's concerned, I'm just an ordinary *peon*.'

'He likes you,' I repeated, 'but if he stopped liking you, what would happen?'

'I don't care.'

'You might have to go.'

'Well, I'd get better pay at a factory anyway. I've been thinking of going.'

The news astounded and silenced me. I saw the prospect of being left there alone – a possibility I had never entertained, an idea so bleak that it affected me physically. I tried to say something, but could not make a word. Chayo responded to my silence by a change of tone. He took my hand.

'Not to leave you! We used to say we were brothers! No, not to leave you. Only, there is nothing else here.'

Nothing else? I thought of the river, our long education, our secrets. 'Here is where everything is.'

'Not for you. You have school. We may be brothers, but you have a father and I don't. He's a rich man. Your real life hasn't even started yet.'

'If that's the case, then I don't want it to start. I want this to continue. I don't want you to go. But if you went, then there would be no question. I would have to come with you.'

'Don't be stupid.'

'My father might fire you.'

'I've done my job. He may take me for granted, but if he considers, if he looks at the garden, he'll see I have worked well for him. And if he takes the word of that evil man over the evidence of my six years' labour for him, then I will go. There is no call to be polite to evil men, even if they are your father's friends.'

'Why were you crying the other day?'

The question caught him off guard. At first he didn't answer it. He laughed quietly. It was nothing, he said; and then he said he could not remember. But little by little he began to talk. Not argument, but fragments. His poor room in the gardener's shack, a cell. His wages which were less than those of the poorest *peon* in the stoniest field. His rest-days spent wandering San Jacinto streets, aimlessly, not even money enough for the cinema, for a book. Perhaps a newspaper. He would read it in the square or in a park. People at war, people with money doing this and that. People at any rate in action. He came home to the garden. An unpeopled world. A hole into which he poured his life. The capital: he wanted to go there. The other world. Here he had nothing at all.

It was not untrue. His room was like a cell in that block of a penitentiary that stood above the scene of our most bizarre escapade. The garden was the lush no-man's-land around it. He may not have been physically constrained, but abstract constraints held him so that in certain moods he might almost have preferred four walls, a fixed door and a certainty. There was no direction, only a fixed pattern to his life – like the flies that travelled about the single bulb which dangled in the centre of his room, tracing their regular, angular courses round and round. So he repeated the same circuit every week: sweeping, pruning, mowing, planting. He had outgrown the satisfaction and pride the garden had once given him. He had seen himself dressed differently, in my clothes, no longer a *peon*. He had learned in that costume another step and another tone of voice. People in the streets regarded him in a different way. And he had learned so much from books. But there was no substance to the part he played. He could not play it on the green island. There were many avenues away from what he was, and yet – constrained – he could not move more than a few paces along any of them.

His mind was rich with indecision. I told him that if he chose one route away, he forfeited all others: they would remain closed to him thereafter. Better to remain at the cross-roads and experience in imagination every possibility, than embark on one road which might well be wrong. Later – and he would be educated then – later he could choose, when it was clearer what he wanted. The capital was a mirage. To rush towards that unknown place would be to squander all he wanted and knew.

'For now, your place is here,' I said, 'whatever happens when you are older.'

'I see, it's all a matter of destiny, then, is it?'

'Precisely.'

'What is yours, then?'

'I haven't got one yet.'

'Neither have I.'

'But if you believe. . .'

'I know why you believe. You can afford to. You're free to say these things because your father's rich. And you don't know. You don't know what I mean.'

He turned his back on me. I had condemned him to 'destiny', yet I did not condemn myself. He defeated me, not by answering my argument, but by implicating me in it. Beyond the walls of this house, beyond our friendship, I knew nothing, except I had been happy here, and though matters would change, I could make do for the time being without looking further. He was not so privileged. The capital for him existed as a place of obscure promise, where he might become the person who wore my clothes naturally and was more than a mere gardener.

He needed more than I. We were unequal. What for me was adequate and final seemed to him provisional. Why did he stay at all? It was for me. And yet he resented his remaining. He used me now, manipulated me, argued with me all the time. Had I used him? The answer was difficult. My father had used him in a clear, definable way. I had tried to repay this use with lessons, gifts, confidence, the risks I took. But these, too, were a form of use. He had altered into a creature more like me, but in one respect utterly unlike. He was one of them, and I was not. His costume upon me fit as ill as mine on him. This fact had come between us and had grown so large, had taken in so much, that we were no longer able to defy it.

Still, I could not accept it. And my care began to generate an increasingly alien monster-brother, all my efforts on whose behalf, all my love for whom, were distorting, distancing – as though the king-pin of my world were being eased out rather than in by the pressure of my thumb.

XV.

My fear that the Reverend Purse would take his revenge on Chayo through my father proved correct. He came to lunch on Saturday. I made it my business to be on hand before the meal and during it, hoping that my hovering presence would inhibit the rector. I was successful, and lunch passed without incident, the rector making himself pleasant to my mother's houseguest, treating her to some of his reminiscences and opinions with which I was familiar already. After lunch, the bridge table was arranged. The game began. Conversation continued, but suspended above the game it became tentative and sporadic, a sentence uttered between bids, replied to a round later, a hovering and shadowy sense emerging. I could, as in a slow-motion film, see the dreaded subject approaching, about to appear in words. But because the game was in progress, I could not risk an interjection. I watched helplessly as the cards snapped onto the table and the crisis drew nearer.

'I was talking with your gardener last week.'

My father glanced up, then indifferently returned his attention to the game.

'Your son was a little late for his class.' He smiled briefly towards me. 'Two hearts.' Then the next move in conversation. 'I asked him about his religious preparation.'

'Oh.'

'He told me he hadn't even been to school.'

'That's his business.'

After an unsuccessful bid, the rector returned to the subject. 'I wasn't criticizing *you*, though he may have been.'

'I rather doubt it.'

I was grateful for my father's lofty indifference. It might yet defeat the Reverend Purse. But I had not bargained for his tenacity in revenge. He pursued the matter.

'No reason you should have sent him to school. He's your gardener, not' – he flashed a smile in my direction once again – 'not your son. It's not your look out, his education. But it's my concern that he should get a little religious preparation.'

'The boy's a Catholic. He goes to church each week with

79

Doña Constanza. I see to that.' His tone was final. The subject was closed. But not for the rector.

'Has he been catechized?'

'I have no idea.'

'I don't believe he has,' my mother said, worried lest my father's tone seem uncivil to the rector.

'It's the Roman church, of course,' the Reverend added, with an emphatic distaste.

'So it is.'

Then, as the rector shuffled the cards before his deal, 'Do you know what he did when I suggested he should come to Episcopalian confirmation classes?'

'Frankly, Purse, I would have thought you had quite enough duties on your plate with your natural parish, without recruiting among the natives. They do very well without us, you know.' He said 'us', but he meant 'you'. The subject was beginning to vex him.

'No doubt you are right. I am sure you are.' The game had come to a stop, the rector clutching the cards, delaying the deal until he had brought the subject home. 'It was a mistake to approach him. The result was certainly unpleasant.'

My father began to realize that, in raising the subject, the rector was not merely making conversation. He was leading towards a complaint, a revelation. 'I imagine,' my father said, 'from your tone that the boy refused.'

'He did not, sir. He did not refuse.' He paused, his face flushed with excitement. He had reached his goal, the point of revelation. 'No, he laughed at me. He chided me. He insulted me. And when I tried to knock a little sense into him, he assaulted me. He pushed me, as though I were – as though I were. . .'

'Just another *peon*,' I said, unable to contain my anger. My father, whose indifference had been replaced with anger, turned on me in surprise.

'What do you mean by that, boy?'

'The rector,' I said, managing not to stammer, 'is not telling the whole truth.'

'What? What? Are you going to take the word of a common *peon*,' he demanded, 'over *my* word?'

'Did you see this incident?' my father asked.

'No. But Chayo told me. There is more to it than that.'

'What more can there be but gross incivility!' exclaimed

80

my father. The rector glowed with triumph. My father saw me as Chayo's fellow-conspirator. 'You should be ashamed of yourself!'

'He had no right! Why did he approach Chayo in the first place? Had he asked your permission? What right had he to lay hands on Chayo? The rector can't even speak Spanish! Some classes he would have given. And Chayo hasn't even been to school!' My speech became incomprehensible. In rage I burst into tears. 'He's fifteen. He's been working here for five years. This man tries to take advantage of him!'

'Go to your room, young man,' my father commanded. But I stood my ground a little longer.

'Promise you'll leave Chayo alone. He's been punished enough as it is. He was sorry.'

'Did he apologize?'

'How could he? The rector wouldn't let him into his sight again. He said he could go to hell. I heard him say that.'

'I don't want apologies,' the rector said nervously, trying to smooth matters down. More had come out than he had bargained for. 'I only mentioned this so you would know. I thought you ought to.' And then, maliciously, he added, 'It's my belief that the sooner you dispose of that lad, the better. Lack of respect and lack of discipline are close neighbours, you know, and they can be contagious.' He glanced significantly at me. 'You must have your reasons, but how you can trust the fellow is beyond me.'

'He's my friend!' I shouted.

'To your room, this instant,' my father said. He had never used that tone with me before. I went. He and the rector continued talking. I locked my door and paced up and down my room. Chayo was in a helpless position. He had no appeal in the matter. He was guilty without trial. If my father dismissed him, he would dismiss me as well. I belonged with him, not with these others who saw nothing but what they wished to see. The Reverend Purse, spilling platitudes at every opportunity, in his bright flowered shirts . . . my father, almost heartless . . . my mother who never spoke except to echo him.

I do not know how long the rector stayed, talking with my father. He was not invited to dinner. As I lay on my bed that afternoon, I could hear nothing but the river and the day-insects. If only Chayo would appear at the window! As eve-

81

ning settled, there was a rapping at my door. I unlocked it. My father entered. He seldom came in there, where my own conspiracy was conducted on weekday nights. I felt like a criminal visited by police on some trivial pretext, when all about him is concealed evidence of his felonies.

'You must apologize to the rector on Thursday.'

'Yes, sir.' What for, I wondered.

'I have spoken to Chayo.'

My heart pounded. I did not open my mouth. It might have made matters worse.

'He will apologize to the rector as well.'

'Will he?'

'You seem surprised. And why shouldn't he, I wonder?'

'What did he say?'

'He said he was sorry. But he said it in such a way that I'm afraid I didn't believe him. His manner was sullen and insolent. Purse may be right about him. Anyway, he'd better do as he said. If he doesn't, he'll hear again from me.' He looked hard at me. 'Do you still play with him?'

What could I say? 'He is my friend.'

'You should get some other friends. Of your own sort.'

'He *is* my sort.' I would have gone on, but my father slapped me across the face.

'Your own sort, boy. Your own nationality, your own language, your own race. Why do you suppose I pay through the nose to send you to a good English school? It's not so you can remain on a level with the gardener, you know. Why do you suppose the Reverend Purse comes out here to see you? You're growing up. It's time you started behaving a little more like what you are.'

He tried to relent then. He patted my head, a clumsy peace-token, as I sat on the edge of my bed rubbing my face, but not crying then, the anger had gone to the bone.

'I'll have Doña Constanza bring you some camomile tea. It will calm you down.' He awaited some gesture in return. I offered nothing. I turned my back and lay down on the bed.

'I don't want any tea. I have a headache. I'm going to sleep.' He left the room, slamming the door after him.

XVI.

Chayo made his apology the next Thursday, briefly, curtly. The Reverend Purse patted him on the head. I made my apology as stiffly. I too received the benefit of his forgiveness. But this incident had changed things. One measure of the change in the next months was my school reports. If '10s' meant a virtuous industry, the '5s' and '6s' I began to record surprised my teachers and filled my mother with alarm. I was becoming 'a problem', my father told me. Though external civilities survived, I became sullen on weekends. Only with Nana did I remain the same. What pleased her I did automatically, happily. But she never asked me to work hard at school. When she heard my father lecturing me, as he did most weekends, she would save me some small treat in the kitchen to console me.

Chayo's work, too, deteriorated noticeably. My father was never content with it. He would pace round the garden, followed by the mute gardener, criticizing every aspect of his work. The spirit had gone out of the boy. If he could not please, his silence seemed to say, he would not please. The rector had managed to damage the whole estate. Each time he came he worked the wounds open again with little asides and allusions. Yet it was not entirely his fault. His invitation to Chayo had not caused, but merely released the tensions that underlay the surface harmony of the green island. There were other, more serious causes, and quite other effects. That trivial incident and its publication had brought only part of the real discontent to the surface.

Chayo's and my escapades began to bore us. He was listless for new modes of entertainment. Sometimes he went by himself to San Jacinto on Tuesday nights. He had tried to 'go inside' with one of the women, but she had laughed at him. He was too young. And besides, he could not afford it. The humiliation merely whetted his appetite. He returned to the lost town often. Once he ventured into a bar there, though only briefly, to look around. He told me it was an ugly sight, men drunk, dancing, propped on stools, asleep on benches;

the women patient for custom, being danced with; the smell of smoke and liquor, the deafening music.

'You would have hated it,' he said. But it had fascinated him, even as it repelled him.

I did not like to let him go alone. But he had told me he preferred to be without the encumbrance of a *gringo* disguised as a *peon*. Sometimes he still took me. When he left me behind, he would arrive at my room at two in the morning, shake me awake, and tell me where he had been, what he had seen and done. I began to experience our adventures vicariously. I joined him less and less. His companion in iniquity (as he liked to call me) had become his confessor.

One Tuesday, when I thought he had gone into San Jacinto, he arrived in my room at his usual time.

'Aren't you on an expedition tonight?'

'I have an adventure for us here, a surprise!' Out of his shirt he drew an object which he placed in my hands. It was a bottle.

'What's in it?'

'Smell.'

I unscrewed the cap. It was alcohol. 'Cane alcohol,' he said proudly.

'That's horrible smelling stuff.' The fumes penetrated my sinuses like amonia.

'Your mother and father drink. So does the rector.'

'Not this stuff! They drink it with water, and not a whole bottle of it. What would Nana say if she knew you'd brought this into the house? She'd rather have a bomb. Get rid of it.'

'We'll just taste it,' he said. Out of his shirt he drew two tin cans he had washed so carefully that the smell of their previous contents was distant and undefinable. 'We'll drink it on the lawn. If we spill it in here the smell will stay.'

'But Nana will hear us. Better, let's just taste it here.'

'We can be quiet. In the open air it won't affect us. Come along. It's nice out. There's a moon. We'll sit on the grass near the window.' He drew me after him. 'You go first.' He followed, replacing the screen behind him.

He unscrewed the cap again. 'Cane alcohol. It costs nothing at all.' He sniffed the cap. 'You try it first, Professor.'

'Where did you get cane alcohol?'

'A vendor at the gate,' he chuckled implausibly.

'Where have you been going? You didn't tell me you'd bought this last week.'

'I must have forgotten.'

So there were now secrets between us. 'Tell me,' I demanded.

'Oh, shut up. Later, man. Now drink.' He sloshed some of the alcohol into one of the tins and reached it towards me. I did not take it. He raised it to my lips and tipped it until the liquid went into my mouth. The fumes were hot and powerful. I coughed and spat. I took the tin from him. The second sip went down my throat, searing it. Thereafter the fluid went down more easily. Chayo drank too, until the bottle was half drained. Then, with an involuntary gesture, I knocked it over and spilled most of the remaining contents on the lawn. Chayo swore loudly.

'Hush. The worst it can do is kill the grass.'

'Come on, let's go into town,' he said in a slurred voice.

'You stand up first. I bet you can't walk straight.'

'Bet I can.'

'A peso.'

'A peso.'

He leaned on me and rose with difficulty, then walked shakily along the edge of the terrace above the jasmine shrubbery.

'A peso to me!' he shouted.

'Shut up!' I shouted back. 'We'll be heard!'

'Now see if you can do it. See if you can walk a straight line. We'll go to town. We'll go to town like princes.'

As I struggled to stand, the alcohol rose in my throat. I fought against nausea and stood. Once on my feet, the triumph was brief. I got to the terrace edge and fell over it backwards into the dense jasmine below, emitting a scream as I fell. The fall seemed a very long way, the landing a deafening crash of twigs and branches. As I lay face up in the hedge below the wall, I could control the alcohol no longer. It rushed up my throat. I was sick, as though my indignant stomach itself had given notice and intended to move elsewhere.

Our shouting had not roused Nana, but my scream did. After the nausea ceased, gazing upward I saw above me, peering over the terrace edge, Nana in her familiar flannel nightgown, grasping Chayo by the scruff of the neck and making him, too, a witness to my fall. I could distinguish their silhouettes against the unsettled stars. I heard her recriminations. Poor Nana. I had committed the worst sin in her book. She floated above me like an angel of wrath. She berated Chayo: about drink, the father of her son, her own father, Chayo's father: the oblivion, the evil of it, what men would do. My innocence, he was corrupting it. She slapped and shook him by turns. I heard this, but I lay unmoving and uncomfortable in the hedge. I felt safer there, nor could I move with any ease. The chorus of cries and shouts above me died down. Since their drama had evidently run its course, I decided it was time to cry out. I announced that my back was broken, I was dying, and other threats, in a choked, feeble voice. I was sick again with the effort and at last, briefly, slept in the shrubbery. Then I felt an arm about my waist. Chayo was lifting me back onto the terrace. He was carrying me to the verandah, followed by Nana.

'You take him now,' said Chayo when we reached the front door. He transferred me to Nana's arms. Through the haze of incomprehension one idea broke, clear and terrifying.

'The door of my room is locked.'

'Of course it's not,' said Nana. 'How could you have got out through a locked door?' But it was. I knew it was. She would find out. She would know about the window, the route of our conspiracy. She would have us at her mercy. She would stop it all. Chayo disappeared and Nana struggled with me into the house. I was heavy for her, and made myself the heavier, trying to delay the moment of her discovery. She dragged me through the living room, down the passage to my room. The door was not locked. The screen was in place. Chayo had saved us. He had run back, sobered by my fall and Nana's punishment. He was an amazingly rapid fellow.

When Nana had bathed me, dosed me thoroughly with herbs, prayers, vinegar and two or three slaps on the face, she left me naked on my bed. 'The air will clean out your head. Never do that again,' she said. It was a hot night, 'May God protect you. May He send an angel to keep you from temptation.' She slapped me once more across the face, then kissed me and left me to the divine mercy. I slept. Then I opened my eyes. The moonlight came brightly through the window. Chayo stood over me.

'Like Lazarus,' he said, patting my stomach which was hollow as a drum.

'Lock the door.'

He did so. I surveyed my body, chalk-white in the moonlight. He came back to the bed and sat by me.

'Are you full of penitence?'

'If I am, that's all I'm full of. I peed all over myself down there in the shrubs.'

'That's not all you did.'

'Why aren't you drunk?'

'I was. It passes. You didn't let yourself go properly. If you let yourself go, you can come back and it's nice. But if you don't, it fights with you and gets the upper hand.'

'I don't understand you.'

'Lazarus!' he said, running his hand back and forth over my moonlit belly. 'You're white as if you were bandaged, and returning from the dead. You told us you were dying down there.'

'Come to bed. No class tonight.' I dozed and woke and dozed. He was there, and then he wasn't. It was morning.

I apologized to Nana. I took vows that it was the first and final time. We lit a candle before her little bedside menagerie of saints to solemnize my oath. Each of those icons was enjoined to keep a special eye on me.

'You must promise me something, too,' I said to her.

'Yes.'

'You must promise not to tell my father.'

She looked hurt. 'As though I would!'

XVII.

The provenance of the cane alcohol was Chayo's first secret from me. There were others. I was filled with jealousy for the unknown life he was creating, from which he excluded me. His rest-days he would disappear to San Jacinto and never tell me afterwards what he did, except in vague, general terms. He was creating a secret area, an unshared privacy. Almost to compensate for this I grew increasingly confiding – not that my confidences were of much moment – and even invented incidents to tell him. He came to the house as before, each weekday night, and I visited him on weekend nights in his room. But when we were not studying, increasingly often we were arguing.

'You speak what you feel, not what you think,' I told him. For moment by moment he would contradict himself, each conflicting statement uttered with conviction, without consistency.

On one point I agreed with him. His work was underpaid. From this agreement followed other thoughts, rebellious and dangerous. The one Chayo returned to with increasing vehemence was the absurdity of the green island itself – a place of luxury amid the general drought, used two days a week by rich foreigners, inhabited – all three acres of it (excluding the new fields where the orchard was never planted) – for the rest of the time by one child and his servants.

Where we differed in our disenchantment with the world we were confined to was in our vision of its future. I said that, given its existence, it should be preserved but made more widely useful – perhaps as a hospital or rest-house, with its own fields and gardens, extending, incorporating the waste land round about. But Chayo, thinking bitterly of the flowering trees on which he had spent so many years, the thickening trunks of the laurels, the daily, monthly, yearly increase in permanence of the garden, was generally in favour of levelling it recklessly – that it should become again fields, like those reluctant stony fields around it, issuing crops when the rain fell. That – or else, in his more sanguine moods, he would see it as a public garden, on condition that he should be sole keeper. In either vision, there was no place for me.

He no longer referred to wealth or race as factors that divided us. There were two new, subtler distinctions. I had a future, he said, whether I wanted it or not, inevitably, by birthright. He had nothing but what he could make by his own efforts. And there was something else. He said he had realized it first at the *feria* of San Isidro, when we rode on the 'octopus'; and every subsequent event had confirmed it. I was unable to let myself go and enjoy release as he could, and as his kind could. I refused to trust the moment of experience, holding something back through fear or reticence. It was not a something tangible, like the secrets he kept from me. It was a secret I did not will, involuntary, which I contained and could not recognize. There was some cold core, unapproachable. This analysis was worse than the earlier ones. It condemned me to difference by something intangible.

'My secrets are of no real importance,' he said, though I doubted him, for why then were they secret? 'But your secret is much more serious.' He was satisfied: it was an argument I could not refute because I was not myself conscious of the 'secret'. I searched hard for it. I invented intimate secrets to tell him, almost asking, 'Is that the one you mean?' Each time he would shake his head. That was not it at all. I would try again, probing myself, to find what it was I could not 'let go', as he said his people could.

It was Nana who one day gave me – casually, in conversation over lunch during one of Chayo's rest days in San Jacinto – a hint of what his secret might be. She had been to market that morning. Chayo had ridden in with her on the bus.

'Where was he going?'

'He didn't say.'

'Where did he get off?'

'At the state college.'

The college was an establishment of further education, the closest thing in San Jacinto to a polytechnic. It stood on the edge of town in bleak but spacious grounds surrounded by a high wire fence. In our early nocturnal expeditions we had circumnavigated it. The only reason for getting off the bus at that stop was to go there – for there was no other attraction in the neighbourhood. The college offered free public lectures in practical subjects, as well as in more abstruse areas such as economics and political science. If Chayo was attending lectures, he kept them secret either for fear that I should be upset by the fact that he no longer found my classes adequate; or else because he was learning lessons of which he thought I would disapprove. I did not confront him with my suspicions but waited for him to mention it himself. He never did. I thought that – filled with new ideas from no source common to us both – he would have to tell me. I should not have minded. There was a sense of achievement in having prepared him for such lectures.

It was simple enough to understand why he had begun to go there. The lectures were free. It was the one entertainment he could afford. And, dressed in my clothes, with what learning he had from me, he could cut a reasonable figure there, among new people; perhaps ask questions, argue back. The image of Chayo, rising to his feet in a public lecture hall and addressing the chair – Chayo, my intellectual creation – made me proud. I only regretted that he did not tell me, that I could not witness his performance for myself, perhaps discussing the conditions of the peasants and the poor without letting on that he was one of them.

In his arguments with me I thought I heard a borrowed rhetoric from time to time. His earlier bitterness had been directionless and abstract. Now it became more cogent and substantial, harder to refute. I feared that I might lag behind him, that I might be deserted, a bird left in its cage while its mate, who has escaped, comes back to taunt it. The prospect of desertion was intolerable. I had made myself a brother. But like Pygmalion's statue it came alive and moved, gradually apart. Chayo wanted to go – without hurting me, but to go all the same. He needed a pretext, and one evening as we lay talking he announced his decision to me. The pretext he chose was the most obvious.

'I'm going to speak to your father. He's paying me half a man's wages and thinks I'm still a boy. I'm going to tell him that I want my wages doubled.'

'He won't do that! Not all at once.'

'Then he can find another gardener.'

'Can't you ask for less?'

'Don't I deserve the wages of a grown man? Don't I do the work of a grown man?'

'Yes – and more. But he won't agree, not all at once, just like that.'

'He'd better.'

The threat hung there until the weekend. On Saturday morning he spoke with my father. I was not present, but at lunch I knew it had occurred. My father was thoughtful and touchy. During the dessert, he broke the news.

'Your friend,' he said acidly, 'has told me he wants his wages doubled.'

'Told you?' I asked nervously.

'Yes, a sort of ultimatum.'

'Will you do it?'

'Like hell. I told him his work had gone off. I said if he promised to work better I'd up his wage by half. But he's damn well got to earn it.'

'He's virtually grown up now. He deserves a man's wage. I bet he'd work the better for it.'

'Grown up? He's only fifteen!'

'They grow up faster here, don't you think?'

'No, I don't. He's turning out just like the rest of them,' he said, satisfied that now Chayo, too, had fallen in with his interpretation of the native character. 'They're all promise at the start, then the laziness sets in, and with it the greed.'

'Surely it's not greedy –' but I caught myself. It was no time to argue. 'Did he accept what you offered him?'

'No. But he didn't reject it. He said he would "consider". He's become a surly devil. I don't know where he's picked up some of the words he uses. After all these years we may be losing him. Perhaps it would be just as well, after his conduct to the rector, and the bad work he's been doing. I'm sure Doña Constanza could replace him easily enough.'

'Replace Chayo? You can't replace *him*. He's as much a part of this place as – as I am!'

'We'll see about that. Don't forget, you won't be here for ever either.'

Chayo had agreed to 'consider'. But he intended to go. He had only waited to give me his reasons. I went to his room that night with one purpose only: to keep him at all costs, by any means. I found him waiting for me at the open door. He was excited with his decision. He had one purpose, too: to persuade me he should go. Hardly was the door closed behind me when he began to talk agitatedly. My father had insulted him. He had refused to pay him a man's wages. Most gardens the size of ours had three or four full-time *peones*. He was doing the work of three men at half the pay of one.

'He says I have a house. I ask him to come and see what he calls my house. He says he knows what it is like, he had it built. He will not come inside. He doesn't say I have worked well, only that my work now is not satisfactory. It's not as though I owe him something. I owe him nothing. If he'd sent me to the orphanage, at least now I'd be a man.'

'I would have missed a great deal,' I said quietly.

'Yes, and of course if you hadn't been here,' he said with a mixture of gratitude and savagery, 'things would have been worse. It's terrible to think. I don't owe him anything. I owe you something, though. I'll keep in touch after I've gone. We'll write. I won't forget.' He put his hand on my shoulder.

I had two plans. The first was the more dramatic and appealed to me. I laid it before him.

'If you go, I'll go too. I'm not staying here alone. We'll go and live somewhere – in the capital if you like. We can work. I can teach or something.' It was the 'somewhere' and 'something' that marred the plan. It was as indefinite as Chayo's own. Like him, I had a desire to move on. The little world we lived in had folded too tightly around us. It fretted us, we needed a larger space. But he was ready to go and I was not. He could go without me. I couldn't go without him – or stay without him.

'Don't be so unrealistic. We've discussed it already.'

'But not like this, not when it is possible.'

'Do you think your father would let you go like that? You'd run away, but he would get you back – and probably have me arrested for kidnap or something.'

'But imagine what life will be like here if you go. Think of me.'

'If I hadn't been thinking of you, I'd have given notice this afternoon, if not before.'

The first plan, then, was unacceptable.

'I have another plan.'

I had considered only the practicability of the other plan, not its ethicality. It was just possible. I could do it for a time. Chayo's wages were small. My own school allowance was almost a quarter of his full-time wage. If I could forego lunch and all my school expenditure, I could add something to the rise my father had agreed to give him. And I could make up the rest from other sources. Vaguely, even then, the fact that Nana concealed the house-keeping money under the bell-jar, behind the saint, among the icons by her bed, was at the back of my mind. I also had my clock which I could sell. And as a last resort I knew where my mother left her handbag each weekend – on the dressing table in her room. There were possibilities.

'I can make up your wages,' I announced. 'I have the means. If I run short, I know' – I added darkly – 'where I can find more.'

'You must be talking about stealing,' Chayo said, laughing with disbelief.

'That's none of your business. But it won't be stealing if it's money you've earned, and I get it from the proper source. If my father won't pay, then I will. This place is as much mine as his, isn't it?'

'Is it?'

'Yes, it is. Squatter's rights,' I said, forcing a laugh. He could hardly argue with me. I advanced the second plan with so many particulars I pre-empted his objections. He had one pretext for leaving: his wages. I would make them up. He still wished to leave, but had no pretext now. He did not like the plan, but its very extremity revealed how urgently I needed him to stay. 'You can see it as part of our conspiracy,' I said. But he knew it was something else. 'Will you stay then, so long as I can make up your wages?'

He considered, and the longer the silence lasted, the more grounds I had for hope. At last, deliberately, he said, 'Yes, I will stay. As long as you keep up my wages. But if you pay me I become your servant, not your friend.' It was a condition I could not let pass.

'How can you say that? You are my brother!' But the anxiety passed. He would stay. I would have bound him hand and foot. I trembled with relief. Without him, what would remain there? The inert books – which with him came alive; the cold chime of the clock – which his presence in my room domesticated; the arguments, adventures, without them life there would be inconceivable. 'If you had never come, it would have been different. But you did arrive. And you must stay now. You see how necessary it is.'

'To you, perhaps. It would be better if I went. We are still friends. We are almost brothers.'

'But you will stay?' And as I asked, I recognized that the secret I kept even from myself was this need. Why did I feel it? It was the unquestionable axiom upon which my world depended. It was the need that came between us, dividing me from his kind and from him. I could not even describe it to myself.

'It's as though you did not trust yourself, as though you were afraid of being left alone with just yourself.'

'No, it's not fear. If it were that, I'd let you go. I could get used to fear. It's something else. I wish you wanted to remain – really wanted to, because you liked it.'

'I have liked it here. But we have said all this before.'

'If you go, I go. But if you stay, you will get what you deserve.'

'I think you like me better than a brother.'

'At least if you were my real brother there would be no danger of your going. But now there is no danger. We've agreed.'

'For a time. For a time.'

This nebulous assurance contained a threat. But in any event our contract had deferred his departure, though our future which before had seemed long and unalterable was suddenly foreshortened, uncertain, a miasma. When I left his shack the next morning, before sunrise, I did not feel triumphant. I climbed into my room, replaced the screen, and turned and looked back towards the volcanoes. The air was clear, and with the sun behind them they were huge – magnified in the beginning light. I felt I was in a fever; and then I felt like a man waking from a good dream, who desperately tries to hold it in his mind, even as it dissolves, and a grey light replaces it.

XVIII.

In the following weeks, I seemed to have succeeded. My world remained intact. But in the seventh week of Chayo's contract with me I saw my own small savings dwindle. In the eighth week they were exhausted. Then began the necessity to steal.

When the time came, my first impulse was to tell Chayo, to lay him under obligation to my courage and devotion. But I paused just in time. For if I told him, and he acquiesced in my crimes, he would be an accessory of sorts and stand to be punished with, or in lieu of, me. My father might seize upon him as a fellow-conspirator or sole architect. And if I told Chayo, what certainty did I have that he would let me steal to keep him? Would he be flattered and amazed, or would he be repelled by the uncontrollable need that sent me pilfering on his behalf?

I began to have secrets as he did. At first they were apprehensions, jagged and irritating, that would not let my mind rest from them. Then there were the deeds which were accompanied by intense anxiety – not that I sinned, but that I might be discovered, with final consequences for my world.

In contemplation, the act of theft was simple enough. My quarry was the money-box lodged behind Nana's saint. I had little compunction about taking that. The saints would perhaps approve the theft, despite the eighth commandment. And it was not Nana's money, but money my father provided weekly for the house-keeping. It was his, and therefore to the purpose. Accident had hidden it behind Nana's saint, beside her bed. But Nana's own savings were safely stowed in a chocolate box concealed in her bureau. I would not have touched that under any compulsion.

The first theft was at once the easiest and the most frightening. It was easy because my victim did not expect it, and did not expect me to do such things if they did come to be done in her own room. I chose a time when the coast was sure to be very clear. It was during the school holidays and it was Nana's market-day, when she disappeared into town

95

for three or four hours' bartering and came home carrying an enormous load of provisions, like a red ant carrying ten times its weight of stone or greenery. The night before my theft I did not sleep, and I kept Chayo awake with intermittent monologues pursuing no particular subject. In the morning I took a book into the garden and waited for Nana's departure, unable to read: the volume lay closed in my lap. She went out later than was her custom. I waved to her from the chair. Her form had grown decidedly fat in the last two years, and she moved down the garden to the gate and the waiting taxi with all the slow dignity of a Doña, as though she had grown into her title as she grew old.

When the sound of her taxi vanished under the sounds of the river and the garden, I went into the house – casually, but as one who imagines himself watched.

The pantry was empty. I never visited that part of the house except when Nana was there, for company or for meals, and the radio played, we talked, and the birds answered from their cages. Now the birds were at half-volume in their wire and wicker cages. The parrot slept. There was shadow and stale smell. Beyond the pantry opened the dark corridor to the servants' quarters. At the end was the door of Nana's room – the door to which I had run for consolation in the first years on the green island. Just inside was the electric bell, still connecting with my room, but never sounded now.

Even in her absence, her own room, unlike the pantry, was alive. It was just as it had been when I woke in it morning after morning years before. Two fat squat candles flickered in front of her icons. San Martin was in especial favour that day. He appeared to have stepped forward, and the candle flame reflected in the bright whites of enamel eyes set in a swarthy face. He had a small pot of garden flowers by his skirts. The other icons flanked him – almost a dozen of them, a tiny army of saints.

Beneath her bell-jar the large icon was still embraced by plastic lilies. Behind her pedestal the box with the housekeeping money poked out unconcealed, such was the trust of the place. Without disturbing the icons or touching the lilies – not even fanning the candle flames – I raised the bell jar and removed the box. It was heavy with small change. There were a few notes in a silver money clip. I chose two of the notes, replaced the box, replaced the bell jar. I was tempted to genuflect with relief – but the saints might have taken that satirically. I left the room silently, though I could have shouted, there was no one to hear. I had enough money to make up Chayo's wage for two more weeks.

Poor Nana. If I could have told her, she might have understood and given me the money. But perhaps she wouldn't have, for since the night of drunkenness she no longer entirely trusted Chayo. It was a risk I dared not take, because if I had confessed and she had disapproved, I would have been unable to steal the money. She would have been alerted.

I was surprised at my own sensation after the robbery. Relief was what I felt, and as I saved for another two weeks my threatened world, it felt as though I were safe for ever. The passage of time was something I failed to register distinctly. If the present was safe, I did not look beyond it. Each time my resources dwindled, the cycle of anxiety and theft began again, but so too, after a successful raid, something like complacency settled on me. My plans were always for the short term, which is the only term I understood.

For a whole month, the money-box held good as a source of income. But Nana – slow to realize she was being robbed, and at first imagining she had lost the cash – was sure to discover the thief at last. The end came sooner than expected. One morning the taxi came to take her to market. I waved her good-bye and went boldly about my theft. But she returned directly, on pretext of having left her shopping bag behind. She caught me squatting before the icons in her room.

'Praying,' I said.

'You! Of all people, stealing from Nana!' She burst into tears.

'Not from Nana. I haven't taken your money.'

'It's all the same. I thought it was Chayo.'

'Chayo is honest. He wouldn't steal money,' I said indignantly. I tried to console her and then began to cry with her. There was so much to cry about. Not least, this source of money was no longer open to me.

'I had to do it, Nana. You would understand if I could tell you.'

'For drink, was it? You stole for drink!'

I couldn't bring myself to tell her why I needed to destroy the house's trust. But I swore by all her saints that it was for no vice, and certainly not for drink. I promised to repay her. I told her how much I had taken. Gradually she grew calm.

'Your taxi must be waiting,' I reminded her.

'Yes, son.' She rose and went to the car, to market, dazed, incredulous. When she returned she concealed the box elsewhere. I would not have touched it again. I had lost an easy source and, to make matters worse, I had incurred a further debt.

XIX.

Still I did not tell Chayo. I knew he would stop me, perhaps depart without further ado, if he knew what I was doing. The situation was so extreme that I was willing to forfeit even Nana's trust and Chayo's confidence, merely to keep him and keep the form of our existence intact, whatever the consequences to the substance. I did not once consider the possibility that he ought to go, I ought to free him, even though he manifestly wished to go. So long as our contract held, he did not mention his departure directly. He waited patiently for my resources to fail. Then he would be released.

Now, with him to pay and Nana to repay, another source had to be found.

Tuesday of the next week I returned from school and took my one valuable, my clock, off the chest of drawers. I opened the little window at the front, through which the workings could be seen in all their geometric complexity. I secured the pendulum with a piece of tape. I gazed at it, silent after many years. I was grateful to it, as one thanks inanimate things when, by chance, they come to one's assistance – the way an old wall might save one from a falling tree, so that thereafter one feels kinship and affection for it. I packed it carefully in a cardboard box and returned to town by taxi. In an alleyway behind the cathedral was a pawn-shop. I took it there, ignorant of its value, and received in return a pawnshop ticket and twice the sum I had expected for it.

When I got home, I repaid Nana my debt in a lump sum. She looked at me, and then at the money, doubtfully. 'I have been saving,' I said. She did not believe me, but she did not question me either. She shook her head, to let me know she doubted me, then disappeared into her room and shut the door. There, in her new isolation, she stowed the money in a better hiding place. The remainder of it went to Chayo.

He was quick to notice the disappearance of the clock. That night, he missed the quiet ticking and the chime. In the dark he could not see that it was gone.

'Has the clock stopped?'

'It's gone to be repaired.'

'It's never broken before.'

'It has now. I knocked it off the chest of drawers this morning.'

' 'You've sold it.'

'Yes.' And then, 'Once you asked me to give it to you. Well, now it's yours, you see, in an indirect sort of way.'

'It was your favourite possession.'

'It doesn't matter.'

'Where did you sell it?'

'None of your business.'

He twisted my arm behind my back. 'Where did you sell it?' he demanded, with unaccustomed savagery, pushing my arm up harder and harder until I told him. 'You must get it back.'

'I can't. Where do you expect me to get the money for it?'

'I'll get it back, then.'

'But you haven't the money either.'

'I'm saving. Where's the pawnshop ticket?' He found it in my trousers' pocket. 'Don't do this sort of thing again,' he said.

'I'll do what I want to with what I own.'

Nana noticed the clock's absence the next day. I told her it was being repaired, and she inclined to believe me. The next Tuesday night, Chayo came to my room bearing the clock, packed in its cardboard box, under his arm. He was triumphant and happy. We wound it and reset it. It was like welcoming home a friend. But from that night on, it was his clock, not mine. 'I'm always here now,' he said laughing. 'Even when I go, it will belong here.'

XX.

Nana did not tell my parents of the thefts. She confided only
in the saints, since she loved me and knew my father well
enough to sense the consequences of her telling him. Better,
she felt, to extract from me a vow before the saints. Each time
I had betrayed her confidence, I had repented, and she partly
trusted my sincerity.

It was fortunate for me that after the thefts she had made
me vow never to steal from her again. The interdict did not
extend beyond that, and so she left me free, without realizing
it, to steal elsewhere without compunction. For her, sin was
particular and penance local.

I had only one further source of money to make up Chayo's
wage: my mother's handbag.

On weekends, my parents occupied a large elegant room
on my side of the house. It was impersonal and cold, like an
hotel room, and smelled faintly musty with general disuse. I
avoided it. In the years I had spent in the house, I had
seldom been inside it, except when my parents were there –
and even then, only occasionally. But now I entered it, studied
the disposition of the furniture. Beside the window there was
a dressing table. When Nana on occasion had sent me to call
my parents to dinner, I had seen from the door my mother
at her table, her face reflected back at me. She would replace
her compact in her handbag, snap it shut, and – leaving it on
the table – come away to dinner. Always it was there.

I considered various strategies for getting to it unseen. The
only one which seemed likely to succeed – and to yield most
– was the most perilous. It involved, not stealing the bag, but
stealing from it, discreetly, so that the theft would go (at least
for a time) undetected. I would excuse myself briefly from the
dinner table on some pretext, go directly to her room, take
money from her purse (but not too much, so that I could
return again), and then go back to table as though nothing
had occurred.

The first attempt was as anxious as my visit to the saint's
money-box. At dinner, my agitation was so obvious that my

mother put her cool hand to my brow. 'Have you got a fever?' she said.

'No.' And then, 'May I be excused a moment?' I went briskly to work. I entered the room. There was the purse. I clicked it open and found an old, delicately tooled wallet, and in it more money than I had ever seen before. I took enough to last three weeks. It was not an exercise I wished to repeat often. My agitation was worse when I returned to table, but I was not suspected, and I had Chayo safely bound for a little longer.

Stealing from my mother was, I told myself, nothing but stealing from my father. The money she had was his. I would not have touched it had it been clearly her own, her earnings, any more than I would have touched Nana's personal savings. So long as I could tell myself, 'It is not hers', I could rob from her, without feeling that I harmed her. For my mother was always quietly attentive to me. Even if she was undemonstrative, I could not forget that it was she who had brought me a new book every week since I had lived there. She must have had me in mind on weekdays in the capital and chosen each volume, anticipating the pleasure it would give me. She handed me the gifts with some small comment which indicated that she had read them, and hinted to me how I should read them. Had my father supplied books, they would have been for edification – moral and practical. But my mother's choice was various and imaginative, and so – without any other notable exchanges between us – she had none the less shaped my mind as much as the English school had done. Quiet and gentle, her presence at weekends had come to please me. Though she spent most of her time, after a leisurely circuit of the garden, sitting on the verandah, talking with guests or gazing at the view, she was a handsome presence. I could admire her, and the way she kept her distance, without impertinence, but merely by a cold formality of bearing, from my father – that I found exemplary. She had worked out her strategy for survival in the households that his money made. And in that strategy I was – though not openly acknowledged – something to be cherished obliquely, with the gift of books, the occasional glance which showed she regarded me in a different spirit from the way she regarded my father. Every week, in the capital I had never re-visited, she went into a shop and chose among the rows of books one book, and brought it to me.

Why did I never steal directly from my father? Always I took his money, but never from him, only from his servants and satellites. The idea of robbing from him directly never crossed my mind. He commanded such entire respect, or rather, fear – for in his power he had it to do as he liked with me – that even to have imagined (which I did not) the cold leather of his wallet in his right breast-pocket as a source of money would have sent me into a fever of apprehension. My temerity did not extend to acts against my tyrant. Instead, his trusted but unloving subjects were my source, and I harmed them rather than risk an act against the very person whose injustice to Chayo had driven me to extremes.

I stole from my mother's purse every third week. On those weekends I dreaded my parents' arrival, and I took my mother's gift with a shaking hand. Still, I felt not guilt but fear of being found out. If only my father had been reasonable and paid Chayo his due! If only Chayo wanted to stay and would accept my allowance and supplement it with my unremunerative friendship! It seemed inevitable that I should at last be discovered. I was exploiting my final resource. How would they punish me? And – more important – when they caught me, how would I keep Chayo afterwards?

All this extortion to prolong what was in any case drawing to a close – all this merely to arrest for as long as possible the fragmentation of a world already, under its patterned surface, broken beyond repair. And yet I could not see why it should change, because beyond a change I could see nothing – nothing beyond the end of it. There were no alternatives. No world had been revealed to me but this one, that had grown round me not by my choice but by its own accretions. And now I chose. I chose to keep it. The consequence of that choice was that things I had accepted instinctively were now consciously apprehended and desired. And as I defined them, they began to alter in their nature, to slip away, until the choice to keep them became itself a desperate enterprise, a continual shoring up of what – the moment the effort of the will lapsed – would cease, subside, flow away. The effort was so total, so intense, that I could not have imagined an alternative – as the believer becomes incapable of imagining a godless universe, his faith being a fact as real as the physical objects and the people that surround him.

Each class with Chayo became more precious to me, even those which ended in acrimonious argument or in one of our fights. The surface held. Nana was there and had forgiven me again. Chayo was there. But it was a slippery world. I could have done without Nana, spared her if I must. But not Chayo. I lay awake after our classes, while he slept, and heard his regular breathing. He seemed to breathe for me as well, and if that sound ceased, I would asphyxiate.

Frequently he asked me where I got the money from.

'None of your business. But if you must know, it's from my allowance.' That reply irritated him. Why was my allowance so generous? I did not work for it. I did not need it. He berated me for my wealth and began to exaggerate his own poverty. At last, one night, I lost my temper with him.

'It's not my allowance. I pay you from other sources. One thing's sure. If you knew what those sources are, you'd stop punishing me all the time.'

'So! You have other secret forms of income.'

'I steal it.'

'Steal it? You couldn't steal anything from anybody.'

'I steal it from my mother's handbag. That, and my allowance. That's where it comes from. Most of it's stolen. After all, it's my father's money.'

'You steal from your *mother*?' He stammered with disbelief. 'Why? Why do you do this?'

'So you'll get what you deserve, what you've earned. So you'll stay. I told you when we first agreed.'

'You're paying me stolen money.' He considered this in silence for some time. 'I think I understand.'

'What do you understand?' I asked bitterly.

'I think you are in love with me.'

'Don't be ridiculous. You're my friend, my brother. I want you to stay here, where you belong. That's all.'

In the next weeks I recalled that conversation. Sometimes his words seemed true. But if they were, they had become so only since he had threatened to go. Before that, there had been no need to define the life we led. Now it was in effect a courtship. I wooed him to stay on. I committed crimes to keep him, against his will. He stayed only in response to my insistence. I kept him by a continual effort of will. And as I

104

made him stay, knowing with increasing certainty that he would not stay for ever, I became clearly aware of what he was, his body when he showered, his physical warmth. I began to enjoy our fights more than our discussions, because they drew us into angry contact. The need for sensation, for the sense of presence, I did not mention to him. I hardly knew how to present it to myself. It was not desire, not the emotion the books my mother brought me evoked. It was just one more complication.

XXI.

For three months my thefts succeeded. They never became easy or lost their terror. Before I undertook them I was almost physically ill with anxiety, a state which my mother noticed. Sometimes I longed for the discovery to come, sudden and final, apocalyptic.

The night of the discovery, I left table on some pretext to commit the crime. My mother had become aware that someone was pilfering from her. In the capital she had watched the servants and everyone with access to the house and had not discovered the culprit. With increasing unease, she began to wonder if the crime was not being committed in San Jacinto, in the heart of her family. She suspected Doña Constanza and Chayo and therefore did not mention the subject to me, lest I warn them. That night, she followed me, shortly after I left table.

I took the money from her handbag and put it in my breast pocket. As I replaced the bag, in her dressing-table mirror I saw the reflection of my mother, framed in the door, stunned and disbelieving. I stared at the reflection but could not look round and face her. I addressed the image as one might an icon. First my lips moved, then at last the words, 'Don't tell father. I can explain.'

'Don't tell father!' she exclaimed, and hurried back to the dining room. She would tell. We had not the sort of confidence between us which bound Nana and me. She would tell. I went to my room and hid the money I had just taken in a shoe. At least this they would not take back. I locked the door. There was enough money there for three weeks. And then?

A furious rapping of knuckles on wood. I admitted my father. He did not speak. He beat me hard. It was a relief not to be questioned or lectured, only beaten, a monotonous recurrence of pain. I could only think that there was no other source of money for Chayo. Even as my father beat me, I tried to imagine some alternative source of money. But I had thought for months already, without discovering anything. I had three more weeks. Then Chayo would do as he had promised – go. If I cried as I was beaten, it was for that, not for the pain.

At last the beating stopped.

'How much money have you stolen from your mother?' he demanded.

'I don't know. Not much. Just a little.'

'You're a liar as well as a thief. And what have you spent it on?'

'I don't know.' Then I had an idea. I might yet escape – and escape in such a way as to get the Reverend Purse in trouble, rid myself of him for good. 'I spent it on church. I wanted to give more at church. That's where it goes.'

'We'll see about that. I'll call the rector,' he said, and left, slamming the door.

I did not cancel my visit to Chayo that evening. I took him the money. 'It's three weeks' worth, so keep it safe,' I said. He could tell that I was ill. We lay silently. I was hot and cold by turns, exhausted by the recent months and unable to grasp the defeat I had at last suffered. I had three more weeks. But what lay beyond them? And I was ill, and my body would deprive me of Chayo's company. In the early morning, Chayo had to carry me back to my room. I was in a fever. Nana came to visit me when I failed to appear for breakfast. She feared I had a relapse of my early illness. But she knew nothing of the events of the night before. My father considered such incidents as none of the servants' business. She confided in her icons, not informing him; and he confided in himself, not informing her. In her worry, Nana told my mother who came quietly at mid-morning and laid her cool hand on my forehead.

'Poor, silly creature.' She leaned down and kissed me on the brow. I was ill. Illness took the place of penitence, and earned from her a provisional forgiveness.

Nana brought me cups of herb tea. The fever rose. I was occasionally delirious, now half-awake, now half-asleep.

The rector and my father were in the room. How crowded they made it. Two loud voices there where whispering was the custom. Large, awkward figures among my tidy piles of books and papers. They were discussing me.

'She caught him red-handed.'

'But why has he been doing such a thing? Surely you give

him an allowance. Most parents give their children an allowance.'

'Of course I do.'

'Tell me, boy, why did you steal money from your mother?' said the rector, leaning over me. I saw his earnest, pink-rimmed eyes bulging benignly, his round face made solemn by curiosity and concern, hovering above me, repulsive, perspiring. I did not reply.

'Tell him what you told me,' my father ordered. I still did not reply.

'Poor chap. He's obviously unwell,' consoled the rector. 'Let's leave him until he's better.'

'Not so fast, Purse.' My father detained him. I moved my lips, but I had nothing to say.

'If you won't tell him, I will. Purse, my boy tells me you have fired him with religious zeal. He's been stealing money from his mother to give it to the church.'

'No! I never said that!' I cried out. 'He never inspired me to anything.' And then, 'It's not his church, anyway.' I almost added, 'It's Nana's church I belong to, not his.' But I caught myself just before drawing Nana into it.

'He certainly hasn't been overwhelmingly generous in the collection,' said the rector. 'I would have noticed.'

'No doubt you would have,' said my father drily. 'Which church, then, boy? Speak up.'

'San Isidro,' I whispered. With that lie I thought I forfeited my favourite saint's protection for ever. I could almost feel his departure from my room, leaving me with only the name to fight off my enemies.

'Are you going to Catholic churches?' My father's rage wavered over me. The lie was the only route of escape left to me. A spiritual conflict, a confusion of conscience, would dignify the crude and literal theft and distract them from seeking further the actual cause. 'Are you becoming a Catholic?'

'Maybe. I'm interested. . .'

He broke in. 'Rector,' he said, turning his full wrath on the unsuspecting Reverend Purse, 'Sir, what have you been teaching my son? For two years you've told me he was being prepared for the Episcopal confirmation. The Bishop is coming in three weeks' time. You have reported to me that the boy was making progress. What have you been doing?'

The rector was confused and angry at the same time. It was a relief to watch the conflict move to another sphere, over my head, between my father and my catechist.

'I have been preparing him for the Episcopal service. He has never even mentioned the Catholic church to me, or I to him. I don't understand a word of this.'

'Perhaps you should have dropped a word or two about Catholicism, sir, to warn him about it. So, I have the church to thank for turning my son into a Catholic and a thief – and a thief who steals from his own mother, of all people!'

'There are other explanations, you know. A thief is likely to be a liar, too,' said the rector. He was disengaging himself, turning the argument back against me. 'Do you really think he is telling you the truth, even now? Let me offer another thought. I warned you once before about the people he associates with. I see that gardener boy is still about the place. I urged you then, and I say it again now, with most sincere concern. Your son deserves a better class of friend. He's impressionable – look how he stood up for that boy's insolence, and learned insolence from him. What else might he not learn? I don't doubt but that the gardener boy is at the back of this somewhere. I'd look a bit further before you blame me or the Catholic church.'

'How can you say Chayo is corrupting?' I was shouting. Anger and fever had defeated my stammer. 'He hasn't got the time. He works all day. And he hasn't got the means.' I desisted from bringing my father into the path of my fury. 'He doesn't go to church now, anyway.' And I added a lie. 'Besides, I hardly ever see him now. Our paths don't even cross.'

'Well, he's done his damage to you already. It's in his blood,' said the rector, nodding benignly at my father.

I sat up in bed and grabbed my father's hand so suddenly that he was too surprised to withdraw it. I gripped it firmly. I startled even myself. I was inspired. The moment for a final revenge had come. 'The Reverend Purse has been coming here for years. All he has done is to spread confusion. I couldn't say this because I knew he was your friend. But I have to say it now. He drinks your Scotch all through our classes. He stays for two hours or more and most of the time he maunders on about his past. It's got nothing to do with God. Please make him go away. I hate him and his church.

That's why I turned to the other one. I don't want to have to talk to him again. The things he's said to me!' I looked so imploringly, so plausibly, at my father from my feverish, tearful face that abruptly all the blame that had attached to me, which I had parried with what little skill I had, miraculously transferred to the rector. My father turned on him, ushered him from the room. It was the last I saw of him. He never visited the green island again, nor did we return to his church.

In the silence that followed their departure, I relaxed. This crisis had briefly freed my mind from the greater problem. I had a sensation of triumph, the satisfaction that a man with a terminal illness feels when he has overcome some lesser ailment – the brief mirage of recovery. San Isidro had assisted me once more. His name had been a bludgeon against my foes and had preserved me from worse blame. I promised him – as Nana might have done after one of her small miracles had been performed – a candle. I kept my promise when, the next Thursday, I was fit enough to go to school. After classes I went to the cathedral and purchased a very large candle. I brought it home with me.

'Nana, may I please light a candle to San Isidro? I owe him a favour.'

'Yes, of course!' In her delight she got out one of her votive candles (she kept a supply for daily use). 'Use this.'

'No, I have bought my own.' I produced my large white candle.

'We will light a candle each, you a big one and I a small one. We will go tonight to the church.'

She rang for a taxi and at dusk we drove to the neat white church with its grey stone tracery and neon cross. It was almost empty. Two or three black-veiled women prayed in the shadowed forward pews. The smell of stale incense hung heavily. That evening ours were the only two candles lighted to the church's patron saint – one large candle and one small. Nana prayed diligently. I looked at him, his upturned, glittering eyes. I said no prayers with my lips or in my mind. If one wants miracles, one should ask only for modest ones. One risked disappointment if one asked that the sun stop, that the rains come, that a person stay against his will, arresting time. I merely gazed at the saint, who in turn gazed into the dark vault. I could not request the greater miracle. He would not deliver Chayo to me.

As Nana made the circuit of the other icons, I lingered at the dim ancient mural of the loaves and fishes. So much evidence of miracles! There, the familiar faces, fed by a benign native Christ. If he would multiply my money, turn those loaves to gold! I had enough now for a week. Thereafter no source existed. My days as a thief were over. I felt I hung on Christ's left hand, without the energy to say, 'Save thyself and save us too' – here, on earth, where salvation is survival.

For without a miracle my days with Chayo would be over. There was one futile last resort: his charity. I could beg him to stay. I had my allowance still. And to this form of prayer – prayer to the living – I attached a little hope, as much hope as I dared.

It flickered as we came out into the warm night air. It was Thursday, and the Reverend Purse had not come! He would not return, ever again. It was one mountain moved. But the joy that he was gone soon ceased. His was perhaps only the first departure.

XXII.

On Friday I told Nana I was ill. I stayed in bed during the weekend. The next week I said I would not go to school. I spent the day following Chayo about the garden. I had a hundred schemes that seemed now possible, now impossible. The nervous fever came and went.

Our classes continued as usual. Though Chayo knew something was amiss, I could not tell him what. I had not even explained the non-arrival of the Reverend Purse the Thursday before. 'I don't know. He's stopped coming.' In earlier days the defeat of the rector would have been a subject for crowing over, for celebration. Now it connected with the end of other things. When, after our classes, he slept, I would imagine his features at rest in the dark. I tried to illuminate them with my gaze, to fix them in my mind. I was awake at dawn when he went about his tasks.

At last came the day when I had no money to pay him.

'I can't get all the money any more. You can have my allowance. You can have anything you like of mine. But not the money. I can't find any more.'

'Did they catch you?'

I told him the whole story then, about stealing from Nana's box and from my mother. About my revenge on the rector – 'for both of us', I said. Then we were both silent. After a long time, Chayo spoke in a whisper, almost to himself.

'Well, I suppose that's it.'

'You must stay. You can't go. I'll go mad here if you go.'

'I can't stay any more.'

'Then let me go with you. Let me run away and come to the capital with you.'

'It's not possible.'

'You can't go, then.' I repeated the words with such urgency and conviction that he recoiled. He did not say he would stay, but he did not immediately threaten to go. 'You have to stay for me. I've done many things for you. Is it so terrible to stay, just a little longer?'

'If it were just a little longer, it would be easy. But the longer I stay, the more you insist.'

The next night he announced that he was going. He was going soon. He would give my father a week's notice on the weekend. He told me after our class, just as I turned away to try to sleep. The words released, like a deep gash, all the anxiety that had gathered in me. 'No!' I shouted. I hurled myself at him and struck him with my fists. He soon had me under control. His lip was bleeding and he spoke in a cold, quiet, slurred voice he had never used with me before, as he might have spoken to my father – though with different words. He sat on my chest and addressed me in the dark.

'It's not money now. I cannot stay, even if your father doubles my wages. I hate the place – hate it. And you – frighten me. All the time you frighten me. Stealing! And now this, insisting, tying me here. You have made me stay too long. You'll realize soon what I mean. If you had let me go when I wanted to, we could have continued friends. You have kept me too long for that. I hate the place. Go see my room in daylight after I've gone. See where I have lived.'

'You have lived here, in this room, too. You have lived here more than out there.'

He ignored me. 'Work for one day in the garden as I have worked – since I was nine. They have used me. But you are using me as much as they ever did. Once you could afford it, and now you can't. So you presume on friendship. It's not friendship you want, but possession. Ever since you started paying me I have despised you more and more.' Then his tone changed, became a whisper full of sadness. 'Why didn't you let me go when I wanted to, when it was natural for me to go? Why did you force me to stay?' He then began weeping, as he had that day in the garden, uncontrollably. I could imagine his face, distorted with grief. I pushed him off me and he fell onto the bed by my side, crying. I put my hand out to comfort him. He didn't shake it off. His face was wet with tears and he pressed it against my shoulder. I could feel the muscles in his face contract and release, his mouth pulled with grief. His mouth. I kissed him. He put out his hand. Not, as I expected, to force me away, but to draw me to him. His body grew taut against mine. He was aroused with hatred, but with memory too. His fingernails were sharp on my back. I could see nothing – a shapeless darkness into

113

which we poured the energy, the passion of six years – spilled out irretrievably. My skin burned, my mouth ached as we struggled, until the frenzy released us and his teeth dug into my shoulder.

Almost immediately he leapt from the bed. He dressed. He had the clock beneath his arm. The screen fell to the floor. Framed in the window, he looked back into the dark room. 'You!' he shouted. 'You!' And he was gone. I did not follow him. I touched my shoulder. It was bleeding. There was no point in going after him. A helpless lethargy came over me. It was an error, it had been an error for months, an error so large that it did not know it was an error. It had coloured everything. 'He cannot go' – and he was gone. There was no plan for such a contingency.

There was an urge to see him once more, just once. I would somehow overcome him even now! But my body lay motionless. Surely he would come back. He would give notice, not run off without a word. He would collect his belongings. But the more I considered, the less likely it seemed. He might come back for some other reason – perhaps to do harm, to show me my error by some act. And I was torn between a desire that he should return, and a fear that he might.

XXIII.

Exhausted, I fell asleep. Had I followed him then, I might have stopped him, have salvaged something from the night. He may have waited a few moments in the dark garden or in his room, in case I should follow. Perhaps he took a few steps back towards my window.

I woke in a chaotic bed. There was blood on the sheets and pillow from his lip and my shoulder. My body ached. As I showered, I thought how little I had tried to understand him. I had clung to his presence, assuming he had remained the same boy I had come to know six years and more before. I had not mastered his changes, but kept him always in the foreground, too near, too necessary to myself. I knew now that his existence did not depend on mine. He was not my creation but a person increasingly perplexing. I feared him a little. I was not sure I could welcome him back. As the warm water stung my shoulder and my face, I shook myself. The crisis had come, and passed, and I was only numb. Yes, I would welcome him back. There was no doubt.

If he returned. For he was absent from breakfast, and in the evening from dinner. Nana went to look for him. She returned in a state of confusion.

'His room is open, but there's nothing there except the furniture. He has disappeared.'

'He has run away, then, Nana,' I said as calmly as I could.

'Run away? Without even giving notice to your father? Without saying good-bye to me? Did he say good-bye to you?'

'No.'

'That's ungrateful and wicked. Why should he have gone so suddenly? And he told you nothing?'

'Why, indeed? No, he told me – nothing.'

I returned to my room early. Removing the screen, I ran carelessly along the side of the house, past the oleander hedge, up the steps to the rutted drive and the gardener's shack. The door was open, as Nana said. The place again filled with its early terrors – terrors Chayo's presence had dispelled. I closed the door and turned on the light. Nothing was there. Not a piece of clothing, not the clock, not a note – no sign I could read, except that he was gone. In the bathroom there was nothing again, only the soap, a thin wafer, half-dissolved in the sink. I sat on his bed. The damp grey walls glistened in the unshaded light of the hanging bulb.

That weekend Nana told my father.

'I'm not altogether surprised. He had changed a great deal in recent months, you know,' he said to my mother at dinner. 'But I'd have expected him to give proper warning. He didn't leave anything behind, Doña Constanza says. But it appears he didn't steal anything.'

'Where do you suppose he's gone?' my mother asked me. She said it in such a way that I sensed she knew a little, instinctively, of what his departure meant to me. I kept my eyes fixed on my plate and shrugged, as though it were a matter of indifference to me. But all night I lay awake again, listening for the rustling of foliage, the silhouette at the window. He did not come.

Next day my father visited the gardener's room to see what condition it was in. 'We'll get another gardener immediately. I'll tell Doña Constanza. If he changes his mind and tries to come back, he can go to hell.'

'He won't come back,' I said with finality as we reached the shack. My father pushed open the door.

He looked about him distastefully. 'What a sty. How could anyone live in such a place?'

'It's the place he was given.'

'He might have made it habitable, at least. Had your friend no self-respect?'

'He had no paint,' I said, 'and not much time on his hands.' We looked around the drab walls, the uncarpeted concrete, and then at the naked bed with its filthy mattress. 'You see in here?' I pointed into the bathroom. 'Chayo's father stole the shower fitting and the mirror, you remember?'

'No.'

'They were never replaced.' I turned on the tap. A rusty trickle of water flowed.

'I see, you think this pig-sty is my fault, do you?' My father chuckled at the absurdity. He was not sorry to be rid of the boy. 'We'll get it painted up for the next tenant. What sort of rug would suit it?'

I was seeing the room in daylight, as Chayo had told me

to. The flies drew their patterns round and round the light-bulb, erratic planets circling an extinguished star. There were cockroach husks large as cigars in the corner. I shuddered. We left the room. My father took a key and turned it in the lock.

'That's that. We'll burn that old mattress, and get the painter in.' Nana had instructions. 'This time it's to be a single man without children. Someone who knows what work is – if any of the natives does.'

'What will you pay *him*?'

'The going wage.' The wage Chayo had asked for and not received. How easy it was for my father to lock the door, to change the world. Casually, authoritatively, he mended his estate. It was entirely his.

A week passed, ten days, without sight of Chayo, without word from him. The possibility of his return continued to agitate me. I desired it and I feared it. I did not sleep, awaiting his arrival.

My fever came again in those ten days. Nana confined me to bed. Her herb teas were ineffectual. I slept most of the day. I kept confusing Nana with Chayo. I called to him. Nana worried and disturbed her saints on my behalf. She hired a new gardener and divided her time between instructing him, praying for my improvement, and attending to me.

My parents came and went, the new gardener got to work, life on the green island continued around me. I lay in bed, expecting and then afraid, for ten days. Then Nana came into my room after market.

'I have seen him'

'He's still in San Jacinto, then!'

'Yes. I saw him in the market.'

'Did you speak to him?'

'I certainly did. I told him he was an ungrateful boy.'

'You shouldn't have done that,' I remonstrated.

'He is a bad boy. I told him you were ill.'

'What did he say?'

'Not very much.' From her tone, I knew she was concealing something. 'He said nothing,' she repeated firmly.

'What did he say, Nana? Tell me.'

'He said. . .' she hesitated. 'He said he was glad.'

'Glad I was ill?'

'Yes.'

117

'Why?'

'I don't know why. I thought you might know. He said he hoped you were very ill. But what is worse, he had been drinking. I could smell it. He was so strange. He was wearing your clothes. Did you give him those clothes, or did he steal them?'

'I gave them to him.'

'He was dirty and very strange. I asked him where he was living, and all he did was laugh. How ungrateful to wish you ill. He wished you –' again she paused, and then spoke the words that most distressed her. 'He wished you dead.'

I didn't care about that. There was only one important question. 'Is he coming back to see me?'

'If he does, I won't let him in. He has no right here, talking like that. He said he was going to the capital, on business.'

'Was he alone?'

'He was alone.'

'Did he say nothing good?'

'Good? He used terrible language. He shouted at me, there in the market. I could have slapped him. He went into a bar and left me in the street.'

I lay back in bed. It was a relief to have news, to know he was alive; and a greater relief to know he was in such a state. It seemed to prove that he was not free, that he had not yet found his way out of our world. It filled his mind still, bitterly. He might come back, even if in anger. It proved he could not leave me easily.

XXIV.

He came one more time, that same evening. I expected him. Hearing the loud scrabbling in the foliage, I warned myself that he was drunk, clumsily making his way along the familiar stretch of wall. His silhouette appeared above the moonlit window-ledge. He did not rasp the screen with his forefinger. He struck it with his fist. It clattered into the room. He stood up on the ledge. In one hand he carried a large object. 'He has brought back the clock,' I thought. But it was a tin. As he bent forward, he poured something from it; it splashed into the dark. Then he hurled the tin towards the bed. The vapours of kerosene rose from the spilled liquid. He drew a box of matches from his pocket, struck one, and threw it into the room.

As he struck it, his own hand, which had been soaked in the liquid, burst into flame. He held the torch of fingers before his face, illuminating an expression I cannot forget, where anger gave way to terror as he saw what he had done to himself. The match meanwhile had fallen into a rivulet of the kerosene, and almost instantly the floor revealed the pattern of the spilled liquid in flame. Suddenly the floor burned, the throw-rug. The bed-clothes caught. With a scream of pain Chayo fell from the window ledge into the shrubbery. I leapt from my bed and to the window. I rang the electric bell I had not used since childhood. I shouted 'Fire' and left the burning room through the window. I followed Chayo, not to apprehend him, but blindly, for some obscure reason.

He had got to his feet. He was running, slapping his burning hand against his trouser leg, crying out with pain. Barefoot, I followed him along the lawn. He headed for the river, down the steps from terrace to terrace, until the sound of the rapids was loud and his cries were lost in it. I kept him in sight, running with difficulty over the rough stones. Glancing back I could see flames in the window of my room. The roof had not caught fire. It was for Nana and the new gardener to see to that. I had other work to do.

119

I caught up with Chayo by the holm-oaks. He had fallen exhausted at the roots of one.

'To the river!' I shouted, lifting him up. I carried him to the water's edge. He dipped his hand in, screaming with pain. He lay on his stomach by the river, gasping for air, his eyes closed.

The river was swollen with mountain rains. In the moonlight the grass bank the water overflowed had streaks and tatters of foam. The water flowed on past us into the dark tunnel of foliage. He let the river suck his injured hand.

'Why did you do that?'

'To kill you,' he said simply, not raising his head.

'But I'm still here. You haven't hurt me.'

'To kill you,' he repeated. He rolled over and sat up. He opened his eyes and stared at me. I crouched before him – pale, barefoot, in my striped pyjamas, beside the river. He might do it here, without fire, using the natural water. The thought may have crossed his mind. It did mine.

'Kill me now, then, if that's what you want. Will that make you happy? Come, you're stronger than I am. And I won't fight back. Here's the river.' He looked towards the frothy water.

'Go back. Go save your house and your property.'

'Nana will have to see to that.' I glanced back. There were no more flames visible in the window. She must have controlled it quickly – aided by the saints and the new gardener. Now she would be wondering where I was.

'Go back. Leave me alone.'

'Why kill *me*? Of all people, why me?'

He had been drunk. The smell was on his breath. But pain and fright had sobered him. I knelt down beside him. He was wearing my blue shirt – the right sleeve burned away – and my grey trousers. He was wearing my shoes, not his gardening sandals. He sat on the bank and held his burned hand out before him. It was an ugly shadow against the swirling water.

'You will be arrested now.'

'They won't catch me. They won't even know it was me. You won't tell. I know that well enough.'

We could hear voices in the upper garden, loud over the river sound, hysterical, calling my name. Nana's voice, the voice of the new gardener, now singly, now in chorus, bellowing my name along the *barranca*.

120

'They will have called the police.'

'You won't tell them.' His scornful voice had given way to a more anxious one. 'I'll go now.'

'You can't go! You're injured. How far can you get like that, with a burned hand?'

'To the capital.'

'You need a hospital.'

'I'll get the care I need. I have some money.'

'They're coming down!'

He tried to move, but he was unsteady on his feet. He stumbled, nearly fell. I put his left arm around my shoulder.

'I won't tell on you, Chayo. You must hide until they're gone. I'll draw them off. Hide here, and tomorrow evening I'll come down. I'll bring food and some clothing – if there's any clothing left! Only, if I don't tell, you must promise to be here. It will be for the last time. You must explain to me.'

'We've talked enough already. What could I say? Get me to some place where they won't find me.'

'Or you could kill me tomorrow if you liked, at your leisure. Only stay – promise you'll be here.'

'No!' He spoke in a tone I could not argue with. 'Let me go now.' And squeezing my hand in his uninjured hand, with all his strength, as though he would grind the bones in it, he repeated, 'Let me go.' But he could not walk without my assistance. 'Leave me over there, in that bank of tall weeds.' I half-dragged, half-carried him along. 'I'll recover and be gone by morning. You won't give me away.'

'I won't give you away.'

I helped him. The voices were coming nearer. I settled him in the deep concealing growth. 'You'll be fine,' I whispered. 'I want to stay with you, but I'd better not. Come back once more.'

'Go now. Leave me here.' He did not refuse to come. He did not agree.

I put his uninjured hand to my face, to my lips, then stood up and left him.

The voices were almost at the river's edge, shouting my name. I hurried towards them. 'Here, Nana,' I called. She received me with angry tears.

I would say I had been frightened, I had run to the river in terror. I would lie – but Nana needed no explanation. She had found me. 'What have you done? I thought you had burned to death! You are safe. Why did you run away?' She kept talking all the way to the house, now angry, now relieved. It saved me the trouble of explanation.

As she served me tea and washed my feet, which were cut from running barefoot that rough way, though I had not felt the pain till now – she continued by turns thanking God that I was well and chiding me. So full of confused relief and anger was she that she did not ask an explanation. When I went to bed, in the strange guest room, where I had never slept before – the room beside my own – the fever I had had was gone. I was calm and very cold, so cold that even extra blankets did not warm me.

'Is it all burned, Nana?'

'Nothing is left. The roof is all. Nothing else is left.'

'My clothes?'

'All burned.'

'My books?'

'Everything.' Everything was burned. I saw it for myself the next day.

XXV.

The next afternoon my father and mother arrived. It was Wednesday. They had come because Nana rang them hysterically and they had no clear idea what had occurred. They were relieved to find only one room damaged.

They came upon me in my charred room, scrabbling among the debris. Fragments of curtain, the familiar flower pattern singed; bits of stinking blanket; the charred pages of my books, and none remained intact.

'Wash yourself and come explain what happened,' my father commanded. His voice was neutral, pending the presentation of facts.

I showered in the unfamiliar bathroom. It had the same view as I had from my bedroom window, the fields, the foothills, the volcanoes, clear again and cloudless, impassive: between them and where I stood were villages and cities invisible to me. Perhaps a million lives, a million men who, if they looked east at that moment, would see the same blue-grey peaks, each with a different thought. I showered for a long time. There were no thoughts in my head. I could formulate no explanation. I did not care to try. Silence was the only strategy worth trying. Dressed then in clothing borrowed from my father's wardrobe – shirt and trousers hung loose on me, and I felt further diminished – I went out onto the verandah.

'Well?'

I shrugged. 'A fire. In my bedroom.'

'I gathered,' said my father acidly. My mother checked his tone with a glance. 'How did it start?'

'Kerosene, matches.'

'What in heaven's name were you doing with kerosene and matches?'

I felt joyful. The guilt already attached to me! They did not suspect another party. The thought of Chayo never crossed their minds.

'I wasn't doing anything.' I would not explain, then. Let them provide the explanation. They had already taken the

123

first step. If I chose wisely in my simple 'yes' and 'no' answers, I could build a story from the alternatives they presented me. They had arranged my life. Now let them explain it as they wished.

They had a theory. They advanced it so cautiously, so tactfully, that it took me some time before I understood them. At first it seemed implausible. But it was the explanation they had chosen. A suicide attempt. And when I saw with what concern my mother watched me, I accepted it as a gift of chance. Yes, I confessed, I had bought kerosene and matches to burn myself alive in my own bed. Frightened at the last moment, I had run to the river, leaving my room, my books, all that I had, ablaze.

How little they had cared to know me. Nana could have told them I was lying, but she was not questioned. And their explanation seemed to account for all the facts they knew. My thefts, my sullenness, my impertinent defence of Chayo all were attempts to draw their attention to me. Poor boy! they seemed to say, and suddenly they made themselves responsible. They bore the blame, as though my father had provided the kerosene and my mother the matches, over the years, the childhood they'd neglected. They cried *pecavi* so vehemently, as though the scales had fallen from their eyes, that I almost believed their explanation. And in a remote sense they were correct, though they spoke from another world.

They inferred rather than inquired the causes. My presence was almost superfluous. They traced their errors back – I ceased to listen, except to the tones which were no longer formal and satisfied but broken by their confusion and self-reproach. They planned a hundred changes. I would be taken to the capital, away from here. I would be sent abroad to school. In that afternoon and evening they dismantled what was left of my small world, like magicians demolishing a palace with a wand – but the palace was already empty. It didn't matter to me.

That night, after the house slept, I left the guest room and the strange bed. I went out boldly through the door, into the passage, and out the main door of the house, down the stairs to the river, the route I had travelled the night before, barefoot. There was no need for secrecy any more. The moon was there again. The river had subsided to its normal course.

Here we had squatted talking, and Chayo trailing his hurt hand in the water. There is where he hung the swing the first time we played and talked, when he showed me how to float out over the rapids. There, the deep, broken weeds where I had left him lying the night before. He had got away. I walked a little distance along the river. I called his name. I was sorry – not surprised – he had not waited. I had food for him in my pocket. I had a bandage to wrap his hand.

Nana told me when I was a child about *la Llorona* – the Wailer – a mother who drowned her child and was condemned to wander along rivers for ever, crying after her dead child. It was her voice, and not the breeze in the trees along the bank that haunted unsettled nights. But on that night there was complete calm by the river. The regular noise of water and insects was all: no human and no ghostly sound. It was a stretch of water without charm and without spirit. The moon spread its grey illumination and dark shadows. Nothing was concealed. A water rat plopped into a ditch at my approach. It was my last visit to the river.

I cannot imagine Chayo's history. I was taken away from San Jacinto the next morning. If he came back, he found no one. I had promised to be there. 'There' no longer existed.

When I arrived on the green island, I do not recollect what I brought with me. When I left, I carried no baggage. And yet I still carry that nothing that I brought away, that insubstantial property I have not been able to lay aside on any journey or hide away in any house I've stayed in.

GMP books can be ordered from any bookshop in the UK, and from specialised bookshops overseas. If you prefer to order by mail, please send full retail price plus £2.00 for postage and packing to:

GMP Publishers Ltd (GB),
P O Box 247, London N17 9QR.

For payment by Access/Eurocard/Mastercard/American Express/Visa, please give number and signature.
A comprehensive mail-order catalogue is also available.

In North America order from Alyson Publications Inc.,
40 Plympton St, Boston, MA 02118, USA.
(American Express not accepted)

In Australia order from Bulldog Books,
P O Box 155, Broadway, NSW 2007, Australia.

Name and Address in block letters please:

Name
_____

Address
_____

_____

_____